Or should she request permission to reveal her boundary-breaking resistance-art to the world? Working in five genres and eighteen sacred modes of persistence, Zilla Novikov submits her third wish. Perfect for your list; instantly familiar; a triumph of optimism. We've all queried, but until now, only the angels of Chelm heard us. Novikov's derring-do opens the gates. Now the world will know.

--Tucker Lieberman, <u>Most Famous Short Film of All Time</u>

A metafictional tale from the publishing trenches, packing poignant queer realism and a fragmented story of loss and climate change, told through wry asides. Don't miss this witty, melancholy story.

--Michelle Browne, <u>The Meaning Wars</u>

This book is a scathing satire with genuine passion and heart at its core. Come for the wit and the blackout poetry, stay for the actual inspiration to fight the good fight.

--Rachel A. Rosen, <u>Cascade</u>

A tRaum Press and Night Beats Book.
Munich, Copyright 2023.

No part of this book may be copied or redistributed without express permission from the author.

Cover by Rachel A. Rosen.
Layout by Rysz Merey.

Query

a novel by Zilla Novikov

a tRaum and Night Beats book

לֹא עָלֶיךָ הַמְּלָאכָה לִגְמוֹר
וְלֹא אַתָּה בֶּן חוֹרִין
לְהִבָּטֵל מִמֶּנָּה

It is not your duty to finish the work, but
neither are you at liberty to neglect it.

--Pirkei Avot 2:16

Zilla Novikov
658 Stouffer St
Whitchurch-Stouffville
Ontario, Canada

Ainsley Lee
Paper Tree Literary Agency

Dear Ainsley Lee,

<u>I wish to marry a man I always love.</u>
<u>I wish to escape.</u>

When Marah does a good deed for a beggar in her shtetl, he reveals himself to be Elijah and grants her three wishes. But she only has two requests. Elijah returns to her six times to ask her for her final wish. Five times, she gives him not a wish, but a story. Each story is set in a different speculative fiction world: dark academia, urban fantasy, steampunk portal fantasy, paranormal-investigation screenplay, and space opera. Each tells a piece of her journey through her new life--her marriage to Henri, her acceptance into his close-knit group of friends. But every version of the world Marah escapes into is falling apart. Can she and her friends prevent the apocalypse before it's too late?

TIL YOUR MOUTH DRIPS (102,000 words) is a postmodern eco-fiction novel comparable to <u>Famous Men Who Never Lived</u>, <u>If on a Winter's Night a Traveler</u>, and <u>The Memory Police</u>. Given your interest in dark eco-fiction with a strong voice and a diverse cast of compelling characters, I believe this book would be a good fit for your list.

As a municipal planner for the town of Whitchurch-Stouffville, I am at the forefront of seeing the devastating effects of global warming on rural environments. It is this perspective which led me to write TIL YOUR MOUTH DRIPS. This novel is the prequel to my unpublished first novel, <u>Fuck, Marry, Kill</u>.

I look forward to hearing from you.

Yours sincerely,
Zilla Novikov

Zilla Novikov
658 Stouffer St
Whitchurch-Stouffville
Ontario, Canada

Lola Alvi
Rosetta Stone Media Agency

Dear Lola Alvi,

<u>I wish to marry a man I always love.</u>
<u>I wish to escape.</u>

When Marah does a good deed for a beggar in her shtetl, he reveals himself to be Elijah and grants her three wishes. But she only has two requests. Elijah returns to her six times to ask her for her final wish. Five times, she gives him not a wish, but a story. Each story is set in a different speculative fiction world: dark academia, urban fantasy, steampunk portal fantasy, paranormal-investigation screenplay, and space opera. Each tells a piece of her journey through her new life—her marriage to Henri, her acceptance into his close-knit group of friends. But every version of the world Marah escapes into is falling apart. Can she and her friends prevent the apocalypse before it's too late?

TIL YOUR MOUTH DRIPS (102,000 words) is a postmodern eco-fiction novel comparable to <u>Famous Men Who Never Lived</u>, <u>If on a Winter's Night a Traveler</u>, and <u>The Memory Police</u>.

You tweeted a manuscript wish list tweet: Environmental fiction, any genre. YA, NA, and adult. With a hint of romance? <3 #mswl

Based on this, I believe my book would be the perfect fit for your list.

As a municipal planner for the town of Whitchurch-Stouffville, I am at the forefront of seeing the devastating effects of global warming on rural environments. It is this perspective which led me to write TIL YOUR MOUTH DRIPS. This will be my first published novel.

I look forward to hearing from you.

Yours sincerely,
Zilla Novikov

```
                                    Zilla Novikov
                                 658 Stouffer St
                              Whitchurch-Stouffville
                                 Ontario, Canada
```

Robert Chase
Alister Tylte Literary Agency

Dear Robert Chase,

<u>I wish to marry a man I always love.</u>
<u>I wish to escape.</u>

When Marah does a good deed for a beggar in her shtetl, he reveals himself to be Elijah and grants her three wishes. But she only has two requests. Elijah returns to her six times to ask her for her final wish. Five times, she gives him not a wish, but a story. Each story is set in a different speculative fiction world: dark academia, urban fantasy, steampunk portal fantasy, paranormal-investigation screenplay, and space opera. Each tells a piece of her journey through her new life--her marriage to Henri, her acceptance into his close-knit group of friends. But every version of the world Marah escapes into is falling apart. Can she and her friends prevent the apocalypse before it's too late?

TIL YOUR MOUTH DRIPS (102,000 words) is a postmodern eco-fiction novel with series potential. It is comparable to <u>Famous Men Who Never Lived</u>, <u>If on a Winter's Night a Traveler</u>, and <u>The Memory Police</u>. Given your interest in topical science fiction, I believe this book would be a good fit for your list.

As a municipal planner for the town of Whitchurch-Stouffville, I am at the forefront of seeing the devastating effects of global warming on rural environments. It is this perspective which led me to write TIL YOUR MOUTH DRIPS. This will be my first published novel.

I look forward to hearing from you. Or not, since your policy is not to respond if you're not interested. But I'm not exactly looking forward to being rejected.

I dread not hearing from you.

Yours sincerely,
Zilla Novikov

                                    Zilla Novikov
                                  658 Get Stuffed St
                              Whitchurch-Stouffville
                                    Ontario, Canada

Amy Bleak
Every Letter Literary

Dear Amy Bleak,

<u>I wish to marry a man I always love.</u>
<u>I wish to escape.</u>

When Marah does a good deed for a beggar in her shtetl, he reveals himself to be Elijah and grants her three wishes. But she only has two requests. Elijah returns to her six times to ask her for her final wish. Five times, she gives him not a wish, but a story. Each story is set in a different speculative fiction world: dark academia, near-future with superpowers, steampunk portal fantasy, paranormal investigative screenplay, and space opera. Each tells a piece of her journey through her new life--her marriage to Henri, her acceptance into his close-knit group of friends. But every version of the world Marah escapes into is falling apart. Can she and her friends prevent the apocalypse before it's too late?

Someone once said that hope is the triumph of optimism over experience. After three hundred and fourteen agents rejected <u>Fuck, Marry, Kill</u>, I wasn't planning to query my next attempt at a novel. I certainly wasn't planning to query you again, Amy Bleak, aka number one hundred and thirty-seven. Form letter rejection, not right for your list.

(At least you didn't say the first few pages of <u>Fuck, Marry, Kill</u> "weren't as gripping as I hoped.")

Maybe I'm an idiot to believe in second chances. But maybe I'll get it right this time. TIL YOUR MOUTH DRIPS (102,000 words) is a postmodern eco-fiction novel with series potential, with someone other than you representing the sequel. It is comparable to <u>Famous Men Who Never Lived</u>, <u>If on a Winter's Night a Traveler</u>, and <u>The Memory Police</u>. Given your interest in atypical story structures and literary-genre crossovers, I believe this book would be a good fit for your list.

As a municipal planner for the town of Whitchurch-Stouffville, I am at the forefront of seeing the devastating effects of global warming on rural environments. It is this perspective which led me to write TIL YOUR MOUTH DRIPS. This will be my first published novel. I'm manifesting it.

I look forward to hearing from you.

Yours sincerely,
Zilla Novikov

Zilla Novikov
658 Stouffer St
Whitshul-Stouffville
Ontario, Canada

Sara Lethe
Bright Spots LLC

Dear Sara Lethe,

<u>I wish to marry a man I always love.</u>
<u>I wish to escape.</u>

When Marah does a good deed for a beggar in her shtetl, he reveals himself to be Elijah and grants her three wishes. But she only has two requests. Elijah returns to her six times to ask her for her final wish. Five times, she gives him not a wish, but a story. Each story is set in a different speculative fiction world: dark academia, urban fantasy, steampunk portal fantasy, paranormal-investigation screenplay, and space opera. Each tells a piece of her journey through her new life--her marriage to Henri, her acceptance into his close-knit group of friends. But every version of the world Marah escapes into is falling apart. Can she and her friends prevent the apocalypse before it's too late?

TIL YOUR MOUTH DRIPS (102,000 words) is a post-modern eco-fiction novel with series potential. It is comparable to <u>Famous Men Who Never Lived</u>, <u>If on a Winter's Night a Traveler</u>, and <u>The Memory Police</u>. Given your interest in #Own-Voices, where authors from marginalized communities commodify their identity for other people's representation lists like they're playing Diversity Pokemon Go, I believe this book would be a good fit for your list.

I'm not a young Yiddish woman from פּלעצל, nor a second-generation Persian-Canadian immigrant, and I'm certainly not a rich white Tory man. But as a municipal planner for the town of Whitchurch-Stouffville, I see the sewer overflows in family basements, the soil erosion on farmland. Every patch of brown grass on a parched lawn, every brownout as the power grid strains to keep up with surging air conditioners, every flash flood as the broken land cannot contain an overwhelming storm, is a siren calling out the alarm. Yet somehow everyone around me thinks they're one-off events. Or they think that technology, that the government, that someone else, that anything besides our own individual choices will save us. It is this evidentially marginal viewpoint which led me to write TIL YOUR MOUTH DRIPS.

I look forward to hearing from you.

Yours sincerely,
Zilla Novikov

Zilla Novikov
658 Stouffer St
Stovetop-Stuffingville
Ontario, Canada

Fatima Kumar
Siren Literary LLC

Dear Fatima Kumar,

<u>I wish to marry a man I always love.</u>
<u>I wish to escape.</u>

When Marah does a good deed for a beggar in her shtetl, he reveals himself to be Elijah and grants her three wishes. But she only has two requests. Elijah returns to her six times to ask her for her final wish. Five times, she gives him not a wish, but a story. Each story is set in a different speculative fiction world: dark academia, urban fantasy, steampunk portal fantasy, paranormal-investigation screenplay, and space opera. Each tells a piece of her journey through her new life--her marriage to Henri, her acceptance into his close-knit group of friends.

Friendship is a strange coincidence of timing, Fatima Kumar. Marah falls in love with Henri, and his group comes for fifty cents extra as part of the meal deal. They're your typical adult friendships--Henri's office mates at the university, crew mates on the spaceship, squad mates in the police division. Bonding as the path of least resistance. Only their world is falling apart. No one is coming to save them. Can she and her friends prevent the apocalypse before it's too late? Are they even going to try?

TIL YOUR MOUTH DRIPS (102,000 words) is a postmodern eco-fiction novel with series potential. It is comparable to <u>Famous Men Who Never Lived</u>, <u>If on a Winter's Night a Traveler</u>, and <u>The Memory Police</u>.

You tweeted a manuscript wish list tweet: A story which strains at the seams and refuses to be contained. Anything which comps to Saramago. #mswl

Based on this, I believe my book would be the perfect fit for your list. I mean, I'm not Saramago. But I'm a postmodern author and I need an agent.

As a municipal planner for the town of Whitchurch-Stouffville, I see the impact of climate change every day. I see the sewer overflows refusing to be contained in family basements, the soil erosion on farmland. I don't look away from <u>An Inconvenient Truth</u>*, which is coincidentally another comp for my book. It is this unique perspective which led me to write TIL YOUR MOUTH DRIPS.

I look forward to hearing from you.

Yours sincerely,
Zilla Novikov

---

*<u>An Inconvenient Truth</u> came out in 2006, and certain workmates claim to have seen it in theatres, but they haven't spent the last decade or so panicking, which seems a tad unrealistic to me.

17

Zilla Novikov
658 Crying St
Whitchurch-Stouffville
Ontario, Canada

Eleanor Jean
R. R. Jackson Literary Agency

Dear Eleanor Jean,

<u>I wish to marry a man I always love.</u>
<u>I wish to escape.</u>

When Marah does a good deed for a beggar in her shtetl, he reveals himself to be Elijah and grants her three wishes. But she only has two requests. Elijah returns to her six times to ask her for her final wish. Five times, she gives him not a wish, but a story. Each story is set in a different speculative fiction world: dark academia, urban fantasy, steampunk portal fantasy, paranormal-investigation screenplay, and space opera. Each tells a piece of her journey through her new life--her marriage to Henri, her acceptance into his close-knit group of friends. But every version of the world Marah escapes into is falling apart.

She and her friends have the power to make a difference. They're rich and connected, they're small-town cops and intergalactic-starship captains. They can work inside the system. But nothing will change unless they choose to act. Will she and her friends prevent the apocalypse before it's too late?

WHY DO I KEEP DOING THIS TO MYSELF (102,000 words) is a cozy mystery, where the mystery is when I'll give up querying. I'm quietly terrified that it's got series potential. It is comparable to <u>No. 1 Ladies' Detective Agency</u>, insofar as they're both books which I think you should read. Your agency bio lists that you enjoy "tightly plotted novels" told from "a distinct point of view" with "dynamic, engaging characters" that make you "laugh or cry." Given that my novel is, in fact, a book, I believe it would be the perfect fit for your list.

As a municipal planner for the town of Whitchurch-Stouffville, I see the impact of climate change every day. I see the sewer overflows in family basements, the soil erosion on farmland. I see the inside of a government which resists change, and I see that, like it or not, those of us on the inside have a responsibility to push until our arms wear out and our hands bleed. If we don't act, if we can't be bothered to walk five steps further to recycle a pop can or to institute Meatless Mondays in the cafeteria or, God forbid, to <u>not</u> build a bypass through the Greenbelt, who else is there? It is this unique perspective which led me to write WHY DO I KEEP DOING THIS TO MYSELF.

I look forward to hearing from you.

Yours sincerely,
Zilla Novikov

Zilla Novikov
In My Kitchen
Making Nespresso
Ontario, Canada

Eunice Smith
First & Last Page Literary Agency

Dear Eunice Smith,

<u>I wish to marry a man I always love.</u>
<u>I wish to escape.</u>

When Marah does a good deed for a beggar in her shtetl, he reveals himself to be Elijah and grants her three wishes. But she only has two requests. Elijah returns to her six times to ask her for her final wish. Five times, she gives him not a wish, but a story. Each story is set in a different speculative fiction world: dark academia, urban fantasy, steampunk portal fantasy, paranormal-investigation screenplay, and space opera. Each tells a piece of her journey through her new life--her marriage to Henri, her acceptance into his close-knit group of friends. But every version of the world Marah escapes into is falling apart. She and her friends can use their positions of power to make a difference, but only if they choose to. Will they prevent the apocalypse before it's too late?

AT LEAST MY COFFEE LIKES ME is a chicklit about a middle-aged disaster queer who everyone is mad at 'cause she can't leave well enough alone. It has almost nothing in common with <u>Bridget Jones's Diary</u>, or <u>Sushi and Sea Lions</u>. Given your interest in dynamic female protagonists, I believe this book was made for your list.

As a municipal planner for the town of Whitchurch-Stouffville, I see the impact of climate change every day. I see the sewer overflows in family basements, the soil erosion on farmland. I see the inside of a government which resists change at both an institutional and personal level. It is this very tired perspective which has led me to write AT LEAST MY COFFEE LIKES ME.

I look forward to hearing from you.

Yours sincerely,
Zilla Novikov

                                        Zilla Novikov
                                             Topless
                                        In My Kitchen
                                     Making Depresso
                                     Ontario, Canada

Skylar Beanie
Pinstripe Literary Agency

Dear Skylar Beanie,

<u>I wish to marry a man I always love.</u>
<u>I wish to escape.</u>

When Marah does a good deed for a beggar in her shtetl, he reveals himself to be Elijah and grants her three wishes. But she only has two requests. Elijah returns to her six times to ask her for her final wish. Five times, she gives him not a wish, but a story. Each story is set in a different speculative fiction world: dark academia, urban fantasy, steampunk portal fantasy, paranormal-investigation screenplay, and space opera. Each tells a piece of her journey through her new life--her marriage to Henri, their wild sexcapades, her acceptance into his close-knit group of friends. But every version of the world Marah escapes into is falling apart. She and her friends can use their positions of power to make a difference, but only if they choose to. Will they prevent the apocalypse before it's too late?

HOT HOT CLIMATE CHANGE ACTION is a work of erotic fiction where I seduce you with my words until you rep me. I would never admit to having read <u>The Claiming of Sleeping Beauty</u> or <u>Exit to Eden</u>, so I'm not comping to either. ;) You have an interest in cli-fi, and while I'm not totally sure if that's climate fiction or clitoris fiction, I've got the novel for you either way.

As a municipal planner for the town of Whitchurch-Stouffville, I see the impact of climate change every day. I see the sewer overflows in family basements, the soil erosion on farmland. I see the inside of a government which resists change at both an institutional and personal level, but then invites you for coffee so you can talk it out. It is this perspective which has led me to write HOT HOT CLIMATE CHANGE ACTION.

I look forward to hearing from you.

Love always,
Zilla (. Y .)

Zilla Novikov
XXX Stouffer St
Whitchurch-Stouffville
Ontario, Canada

Nora Parker
Fever Dreams LLC

Dear Nora Parker,

```
           ,;;,
         6!9999!!6
         69,,,,,,!,
          9,,,,,,,69;
          ,!,,,!!,,!!
          ;9,,,,!!!9,
          69,,,,,,99,
          !!,,,,,,,?,
           9,,,,,,,,!,
          ,96,,,,,,,!!
          ,!!9,,,,,!!!
          9!?,,,,,,!!!
          ;?9!,,,,,,,!,
          9!,,,,,,,,,9;
          ,!,,,,,,,,,,9
        69,,,,,!,,,,,9;
       ,9,,,,,,!9!,,,,96
       !!,,,,,,,,,,,,,,96
      ,?,,,,,,,,,!,,,,,9;
      ,?,,,,,,,,,?!,,,,!!
      9,,,,,,,,6?!,,,,,96
      ,!!,!!,,,,99,,,,!!6
       ,66,,6;;6,,,6;,
```

Please rep me.

Yours sincerely,
Zilla Novikov

Zilla Novikov
658 Stouffer St
Whitchurch-Stouffville
Ontario, Canada

Jennie Wong
Between the Lines LLC

Dear Jennie Wong,

<u>I wish to marry a man I always love.</u>
<u>I wish to escape.</u>

When Marah doe<u>S</u> a good deed for a beggar in her shtetl, he reveals himself to be Elijah and grants her three wishes. But she only has two req<u>U</u>ests. Elijah returns to her six times to ask her for her final wish. Five times, she gives him not a wish, <u>B</u>ut a story. Each story is set in a different speculative fiction world: dark academia, urban fantasy, steampunk porta<u>L</u> fantasy, paranormal-investigation screenplay, and space opera. Each tells a piece of her journey through her new l<u>I</u>fe--her <u>M</u>arriage to Henri, her acceptance into his close-knit group of friends. But every version of the world Marah escapes into is falling apart. She and her friends can use the<u>I</u>r positions of power to make a difference, but only if they choose to.

Her friends are<u>N</u>'t bad people, Jennie Wong. They want to do the right thing. But everyday life has so many demands on our attention, a cacophony of minor crises. The nebuliser blows in the space ship's engine room, an epidemic of j<u>A</u>ywalking requires urgent police attention. There's always another here-and-now in the way of then. Can they get their shit together and prevent the apoca<u>L</u>ypse before it's too late?

TIL YOUR MOUTH DRIPS (102,000 words) is a post-Modern eco-fiction novel with seriEs potential. A careful study of my Amazon recommendations SuggestS it is comparable to <u>Famous Men Who Never Lived</u>, <u>If on a Winter's Night a Traveler</u>, <u>And The Memory Police</u>, but I can't lie to you, Jennie WonG, I've never read any of them. I have a very full life and I couldn't fit it into my busy schedule. Given that they're on your wish list, I bet you have. Do you think you could request my full and tell me if they're similar?

As a municipal planner for the town of Whitchurch-Stouffville, I see the impact of climate change every day. Everyone who works here does. Eric might be a bit useless in Transport, but he doesn't want hIs unconceived future children to drown or burn or starve. He's promised to work with me on Meatless Mondays, and he and Bronwyn iNvited me to their engagement party.

I look forward to hearinG from you.

Yours sincerely,
Zilla Novikov

Zilla Novikov
658 Stouffer St
Whitchurch-Stouffville
Ontario, Canada

Tom Wilson
R. R. Jexion Literary Agency

Dear Tom Wilson,

I reveal a story of falling apart. it's too late a postmodern Memory

I look forward ▮▮▮▮▮▮▮▮▮▮▮.

Yours sincerely,
Zilla Novikov

Zilla Novikov
A Fictional Version of
Whitchurch-Stouffville
Ontario, Canada

Stephanie D'Arcy
Creative Arts and Crafts

Dear Stephanie D'Arcy,

This is a story about Chelm, but it's not a funny story.

There is a town in Poland called Chelm, north of Zamosc and south of Biala Podlaska, only sixteen miles from the Ukraine border. The inhabitants of this Chelm are no more or less sensible, on the whole, than you find in any city. This Chelm was vibrant and multicultural and bustling with Jews, until World War II came along and, as Wikipedia blandly describes it, homogenized the population. This isn't a story about that Chelm.

This story is about כעלם, the Chelm that existed in the imagination of European and diaspora Jews; the Chelm where Yiddish foolish tales were set, familiar stories told and retold by generations of Jews. This is the Chelm that an angel flew over with a burlap sack of fools, intending to divide the lot fairly between humanity. Only the angel was a bit tired, maybe still feeling the effects of one too many glasses of schnapps the night before, and he flew too low. The bag snagged on Chelm Hill and tore open, and out fell all the fools in one place. The angel wanted to fix his mistake, of course, but what is done is done. By the time he got down to Earth, the people had already built a shul, and a cheder, and named their village Chelm. What could he do? He flew on and left the Jews there undisturbed, where they bumbled their way through life making every kind of mistake, and somehow got through from Yom Kippur to Rosh Hashanah no wiser than they were the previous year. But they got through as much as anyone did.

These are the opening lines of (102,000 words) אל אני בוס ועליח 80 אלו ר'עולש ןעלי ולאנצר ןולא

my postmodern eco-fiction novel with series potential. It might be comparable to <u>The Yiddish Policemen's Union</u>, <u>Most Famous Short Film of All Time</u>, and <u>A + E</u> (a novella), but then again it might not.

You liked my tweeted pitch during the Twitter pitch party #pitdark:

PoMo Spec Eco-Fic Novel
-Night Beats in every verse
-Fairytale AU
-Coffee shop AU
-Superhero AU
-Steampunk dystopia AU
-AU where they're cops who investigate the strength of their feelings
-Space opera AU
-Fuck genre boundaries
-Maybe literally
#pitdark #a #lf #sf

The pitch was a bit offbeat, but so is my book אל אני בוס ועליח 80 אלו ר'עולש ןעלי ולאנצר ןולא.
Your agency bio is bland and uninspiring, no offence intended, Stephanie D'Arcy, but you liked my tweet despite that. Maybe, under the sur-

face, you're a bit offbeat too. Maybe you and my novel will get along just fine.

As a municipal planner for the town of Whitchurch-Stouffville, I see the impact of climate change every day. The system might be a foolish one, but it's all we've got, and I'm one of a small group of thoughtful, committed citizens working to make a difference from inside it. I'm chronicling our journey through metaphor and theme in *[handwritten note in unknown script]*

I look forward to hearing from you.

Yours sincerely,
Zilla Novikov

Zilla Novikov
658 Positive Vibes Only Ln
Whitchurch-Stouffville
Ontario, Canada

Edmund Beech
Eleven Manuscripts LLC

Dear Edmund Beech,

Don't look, Liza told herself. Nothing good ever came from checking. It was always better to embrace ignorance than unhappiness. Of course, that's not how the mind worked. The instinct followed immediately from the thought. Wanting to look was the same thing as looking.

Six days, twenty hours. More or less.

It wasn't exact. She'd been off in her estimates before, thinking the mall was a half an hour walk instead of forty-five minutes. Expecting Marah to text on Tuesday and it turned out to be Monday. Her mind wasn't a scientific instrument. She had those, could have lowered the error, but she wasn't enough of a fool to demand precision on a question that she should never have asked. After all, whatever Skye says now, however sweet and kind and accepting she seems, in six days this is done and Skye's gone. Don't tell her your promises or your plans. Don't break your own heart.

Unless she went into this without expecting forever. Life was about working with what you had and what Liza had was a very pleasant companion for almost a week. This was an opportunity. Liza could live a rom-com montage. All the trappings of new love, and none of the risk, since unlike the fools in a thousand movies, she wasn't going in blind. Six days. Twenty hours.

Step one of the montage was breakfast. She shook Skye's shoulder, ignoring the adorable way the girl clutched at the pillows and burrowed into the sheets to escape the pressure. Liza shifted her weight so she was on top of Skye and shook her again, gently persistent. "Get up, already. We're missing the breakfast specials." Thirteen minutes, forty-seven seconds. "How fast can you get dressed? We'll make it if we run."

Skye stretched, a momentary confusion at the woman in bed with her, at the location of the bed itself, before the previous night filtered through her consciousness. "Mmph." She yawned and rubbed a palm against her eyes. She looked delightful, and Liza planted a kiss on her morning breath. "Breakfast. Yes. Good idea." Skye's eyes scanned the floor until she found the sequined dress abandoned there. Six hours, four minutes ago. "Got any clothes I can borrow?"

These are selected lines from my postmodern eco-fiction novel PRIDE AND POLLUTION (102,000 words). It is comparable to <u>The Sleep of Reason: Cascade</u>, <u>The Sleep of Reason: Blight</u>, and <u>The Sleep of Reason: Braid</u>.

You liked my tweeted pitch during the Twitter pitch party #pitdark:

a partial list of tropes
-Love at first sight
-Meet cute
-Fish out of water
-Friends to lovers
-Rivals to lovers
-Lovers to lovers

-Five times Marah told a story (and one time she didn't)
#pitdark #a #lf #sf

It's possible that your finger slipped when you clicked that little red heart on my tweet, but I'm going to engage in conscious optimism. I choose to be hopeful. PRIDE AND POLLUTION is perfect for your list.

As a municipal planner for the town of Whitchurch-Stouffville, I see the impact of climate change every day. I'm one of a small group of thoughtful, committed citizens working to make a difference, if only to save our much-loved minigolf clubhouse from another sewage-related incident. All politics is local, Edmund Beech, and that's the kind of human story I'm telling in PRIDE AND POLLUTION.

I look forward to hearing from you.

Yours sincerely,
Zilla Novikov

Zilla Novikov
A Fictional Version of
Whitchurch-Stouffville
Would Be Better
Ontario, Canada

Travis Tracks
Hope Killer Literary Agency

Dear Travis Tracks,

The apocalypse revealed itself in absences. Nutella became extravagantly expensive and flew off the shelves, an unsightly gap in the breakfast aisle till the ubiquitous strawberry jam took its place. There was a week of wild speculation where a gallon of hazelnuts cost more than the same of oil, before Ferrero reformulated the recipe using almonds, and Midwestern farmers propagated new orchards to replace the ones lost in Turkey, and things went on much as they had before.

A town in France disappeared. This place held no particular importance to global trade, but four hundred or so years ago Henri's ancestors left Aubagne for Marseille, and from there, they boarded a ship to New France. The town was full of living people, fifty-thousand lives gone in the blink of an eye, but it was also a piece of history, a memory, and that was gone too.

Henri's PhD supervisor, Dr Reid Curtis, was an absence, a smile in the shape of a man.

These are selected lines from my postmodern eco-fiction novel HEY HEY HEY DID YOU NOTICE THAT THE WORLD IS ENDING? (102,000 words). It is comparable to <u>How to Save Our Planet: The Facts</u>, or perhaps to <u>Melancholic Parables</u>, which is what's going to happen if you don't read the first comp. Given your interest in inspiring Christian YA and MG, you are a terrible fit for my book, but somehow this query ended up in your inbox regardless. Sorry.

As a municipal planner for the town of Whitchurch-Stouffville, I see the impact of climate change every day. I also see the civil servants who claim to give a shit but then for their engagement party they serve tiny triangles of roast beef sandwiches on single-use plates, and there are fucking orange and white striped plastic straws in the iced tea Bellinis. It is this immense frustration which has led me to pen HEY HEY HEY DID YOU NOTICE THAT THE WORLD IS ENDING?

I look forward to very little about social interactions.

Yours sincerely,
Zilla Novikov

Zilla Novikov
658 Stouffer St
Whitchurch-Stouffville
Mostly Harmless

Dylan Grant
Lloyd McMaster & Co.

Dear Dylan Grant,

Gita liked simplicity. Sitting in the control room of a short-haul flyer with a couple of black-market lasers screwed on was a dangerous place to be when the Empire's Cleaners showed up. But it wasn't complicated. She checked her sights and mentally adjusted down a few notches to compensate for the rush job she'd made of installing the weapons. Satisfied, she looked around the narrow cabin. Marah's cheeks were wet. Caspian's weren't. Henri looked calm and unconcerned, which was a very bad sign. Gita knew his tells.

She shot him a razor-thin smile. "We could wait for them to fire first." She didn't give him time to respond before she hit the button.

These are selected lines from my postmodern eco-fiction novel A WORKING GIRL'S GUIDE TO OVERFLOWING BASEMENTS (102,000 words). It is comparable to <u>The Hitchhiker's Guide to the Galaxy</u>, <u>The Restaurant at the End of the Universe</u>, <u>Life, the Universe and Everything</u>, <u>So Long, and Thanks for All the Fish</u>, and <u>Mostly Harmless</u>. Given your interest in dark, self-aware humour, I think my novel is perfect for your list.

As a municipal planner for the town of

Whitchurch-Stouffville, the only thing I could get at the cafeteria for Meatless Mondays was a garden salad. On my way back from the chip truck, I ran into the usual motley crew of protesters outside Town Hall. A short girl with perfectly winged black eyeliner--young woman I guess, she looked university age--held a placard in one hand and struggled to keep her side of a multicoloured banner level with that of the tall red-haired woman on the other end. The student's placard was that meme of the dog with coffee, surrounded by fire, only the dog was saying, THIS IS NOT FINE. The banner read NO GREENBELT BYPASS.

There's a group of them outside the offices every Monday. The individuals change from week to week, but these four are regular repeats and I recognized them, the way even a stranger becomes familiar with repetition. I usually avoid eye contact when I walk past them, lest I be saddled with a tree-worth of leaflets, but that day I couldn't help myself from saying, "'You can't win, you know. You can't lie in front of the bulldozer indefinitely.'"

I don't know why I said it. I'm more Slartibartfast than Prosser.

I guess I was saying it to the dark-haired man with the green baseball cap holding the sign that said, WINTER IS NOT COMING, since he was the first to laugh. It was the other redhead, a man just as tall and lanky as the banner-bearing woman, who answered me. I know it's unrealistic to have two gingers in a group of less than a half dozen, but that's nonfiction for you. "'We'll see who rusts first,'" he said. I snorted and he added, "You could lie down in the mud in front of the bulldozer instead of us." There was the barest hint of a Newfoundland accent buried under the bland Ontario tones.

"And you'll go to the pub while I do?" I asked. "Have a pint to toast the end of the world?"

"There's plenty of room at the pub," said the redhead woman. "And the bulldozer isn't going anywhere today. You should come along."

I shook my head and shrugged towards the Town Hall. "My boss frowns on midday drinking, and I have mountains of spreadsheets to process." Honestly, I've never seen anyone get fired from a government job, and I wouldn't have been the first to engage in a spot of day drinking. Bill in Zoning regularly fails to make it back to the office after a liquid lunch, and as long as he promises not to do it again, his job is safe. The firing process is a lot of work for management. But some poor residents are going to come up-close and personal with a load of sewage if I don't get my work done. "Maybe next time."

I don't know why I said that either.

"You can come to our meeting instead? It's after work hours, at 7. On Thursday, in the Quaker Meeting House in Newmarket," the eyeliner-student said, placing a leaflet in my unresisting hands.

I'm looking forward to it.

Yours sincerely,
Zilla Novikov

Zilla Novikov
658 Stouffer St
A Foolish Town in
Ontario, Canada

Ivonne Newpen
Paige Turner Literary Agency

Dear Ivonne Newpen,

Marah, who lived an ordinary existence, had never thought herself to be the sort of person to be granted a wish, let alone three. But all women pray, and what is a wish but a prayer with a middleman? Marah trusted Elijah, as well she might. Still, she exhaled a long, quiet breath before she spoke.

"I wish to marry a man I always love."

There was sorrow in Elijah's dark eyes when he answered her. "If that is your first wish, it will be." He clasped his hands together. "What is your second wish?"

There was a long moment of silence. Marah's voice was nearly inaudible as she uttered a wish she'd never spoken aloud, a prayer she'd barely dared to whisper in her own head. Marah was a sensible girl, and she prayed that her father would get a good price for his twisted ropes, that her mother could make the borscht stretch for another meal. She never wasted her words on the impossible. "I wish to escape."

These are selected lines from my postmodern eco-fiction novel SPREADSHEETS FOR ANARCHISTS (102,000 words). This book is comparable to <u>How the Wise Men Got to Chelm: The Life and Times</u>

of a Yiddish Folk Tradition, Yiddish Folktales (The Pantheon Fairy Tale and Folklore Library), and בײַטל מעשׂה . Given your interest in speculative fiction-folktale mashups, I think my novel is perfect for your list.

Thursday was fun.

In the interests of full disclosure, I need to acknowledge that Thursday's meeting was excruciatingly dull. They were discussing Pass the Mic, which is about platforming local Indigenous voices in the activist movement. It seems like a no-brainer, right, Ivonne Newpen? The seventeen people in the room seemed to think so, since everyone used their time to speak in favour of the proposal, even though Isabella from the Mississaugas of the Credit had already covered everything when she presented the idea in the first place. The meeting still took over an hour for sixteen people to agree with her, and they had to push back planning around the Premier's visit till next week.

Don't get me wrong, it was miles better than the Council meeting getting ready for his visit. I don't regret skipping minigolf with Eric and Bronwyn for it.

The group passed a hat around after. Not a literal hat, thank goodness--Jonah's baseball cap might be the only thing protecting the world from his unruly mass of black hair. They asked for donations to cover the utilities for the room, and I guess I never thought about who pays for this kind of thing. It's not like Council has a budget line for protest movements. I put in a twenty but I have no idea if that was the right amount?

Sujay caught me loitering awkwardly by the door, trying to figure out the post-meeting etiquette. I was right about her age--she finished an undergrad in Communications last year, and she's working at a coffee shop and crashing on Ian's couch while she tries to find something meaningful to do with her existence.

"Do you want tea or coffee? Sorry, no. Ian broke the coffeemaker and no one's been able to fix it. He can't be trusted around advanced technology like a coffee machine." Sujay didn't leave me time to refuse, deftly guiding me to a kettle, a stack of brown-stained mugs, and a clear jar half full of white tea bags. I reached for a Nanaimo bar and she shook her head. "Eat at your own risk. Blythe made those and she's an easily distracted biologist."

I ate three and I'm not dead yet.

I look forward to your response.

Yours sincerely,
Zilla Novikov

Zilla Novikov
658 Cres Ln Rd Ave St
Whitchurch-Stouffville
Ontario, Canada

Algernon Hallbergmoos
Witless & Co Literary Agency

Dear Algernon Hallbergmoos,

The sea floor rumbled beneath them, the sound of gears winding past the limits of their springs. The hissing scream of fire against water. The deep, throaty growl of a life awakening.

Skye dropped to her knees and pressed her face to the round glass window on the bottom of the submersible, held her breath so she wouldn't fog her sight. Beside her, Marah whispered, "Borekh Hashem," and Gita said nothing at all. The magma glowed dull red as it emerged from the sliding edges of separating tectonic plates, blazed into furious glory as it took shape and a dragon crystallised into existence. She could hear the tick tock of a clockwork heart beginning to beat, and she thought her own heart might burst from wonder.

These are selected lines from my postmodern eco-fiction novel EXPECT LESS (102,000 words). It is comparable to <u>Robert's Rules of Order</u>, or rather to <u>Tear and Share</u>, which is what is going to happen to that if I ever get hold of a paper copy. Given your interest in unique literary structures and wordplay, I'm 90% sure my book is a good fit for your list. 75%. 49% but I'm feeling lucky.

I have a question for you, Algernon Hallbergmoos. Have you ever stopped to think about the history of the structures that underpin your existence? Have you ever wondered about the classism and ableism of Strunk & White's <u>Elements of Style</u> or the colonialism inherent in <u>Robert's Rules of Order</u>? I bet you haven't, Algernon Hallbergmoos, and shame on you for that omission. Shame on you.

Which is to say, the Thursday evening meetings are continuing more-or-less apace. Last night they debated whether Police Liaisons should have armbands or be cancelled as problematic. You'd think there could be some middle ground, Algernon Hallbergmoos. They could get both an armband and a stern lecture about the perils of collaboration. I didn't suggest this to the group, since we were running late enough as it was, but I thought it very loudly. We never made it to the discussion point on training more Legal Observers, but I'm sure it will make for an equally scintillating Thursday night when we get there.

Jonah was stacking up chairs after the meeting, and it seemed like the thing to do, so I joined in. Jonah--and Blythe--are both Métis Nation of Manitoba. Until I met them I didn't know Métis had a nation, no thank you to my grade 10 history class, which is the first and last time I learned about Métis people during formal education. "Zilla," he said, and full marks to him for remembering. "We met at Town Hall, right?"

"Yeah," I replied, doing my part to contribute to the scintillation level of the conversation. I'd been introduced to everyone the first week, but small talk isn't at the top of my skill set. "Yeah, that was me."

"You work for the city?" he asked, taking the chairs off my hands and shooting a crooked grin my way. Jonah is compact the way a grenade is compact, full of potential energy, unwilling to stay contained. His dark brows furrow when he's listening to you and the glint in his eye reminds me of the man your mother meant when she told you to beware of handsome rogues. I assume she told you that, Algernon Hallbergmoos. I don't know.

"Yeah," I said again. He was looking me over, assessing me for something, and I was mostly sure he wasn't about to deliver a stern lecture. Mostly.

"So you know how to write?" There's no way he realized what a great, lifestyle-affirming question he'd asked, unless he moonlit as an agent under a fake name. I don't talk about my fiction.

"A bit," I said, with completely unnecessary modesty. <u>Fuck, Marry, Kill</u> is a masterpiece and EXPECT LESS is even better. "Reports and stuff."

"That's great," he said, and I definitely did not give myself an internal high-five. That would have caused organ damage. "Do you think you could join Ian and Sujay on Media? Sujay's got social media covered, but Ian--" He looked conspiratorially at me. "Spell check doesn't help when you mix up public and pubic. Or election and erection. I don't know how it missed festivities and festitties, but--" He shrugged and I laughed. "Sujay could use some backup."

"Sure thing," I said, attempting, and failing, to play it cool. The overlap between my skill

set and activism might be minimal, but this, I
could do. "Sounds fun."

I look forward to hearing from you.

Yours sincerely,
Zilla Novikov

Zilla Novikov
658 Stouffer St
Whitchurch-Stouffville
Ontario, Canada

[Agent]
[Agency]

Dear [Agent],

<u>I wish to marry a man I always love.</u>
<u>I wish to escape.</u>

When Marah does a good deed for a beggar in her shtetl, he reveals himself to be Elijah and grants her three wishes. But she only has two requests. Elijah returns to her six times to ask her for her final wish. Five times, she gives him not a wish, but a story. Each story is set in a different speculative fiction world: dark academia, urban fantasy, steampunk portal fantasy, paranormal-investigation screenplay, and space opera. Each tells a piece of her journey through her new life--her marriage to Henri, her acceptance into his close-knit group of friends. But every version of the world Marah escapes into is falling apart. Can she and her friends prevent the apocalypse before it's too late?

TIL YOUR MOUTH DRIPS (102,000 words) is a postmodern eco-fiction novel comparable to <u>Famous Men Who Never Lived</u>, <u>If on a Winter's Night a Traveler</u>, and <u>The Memory Police</u>. Given your interest in [the genre/adapt for agent], I believe this book would be a good fit for your list.

You must know Lola Alvi since you both work

at the same agency. I'm only querying you now because I got a rejection from Lola Alvi this morning. Authors can't query two agents from the same agency at the same time.

There are a lot of rules for authors, Rufus Homan.

Lola Alvi sent me a form response where she wrote that the first few pages of TIL YOUR MOUTH DRIPS "weren't as gripping as I hoped." Authors are supposed to personalize our letters.

I went for a walk and a coffee after I got the e-mail. Sujay was behind the counter and she layered on the chocolate shavings when she saw I was upset, even though I said I didn't want to talk about it and besides, that's not traditionally part of a cappuccino. Ian was there too, sitting in the corner by the window, doing whatever on his laptop. I still haven't figured out what his actual job is.

They started talking about Jordan's plea for Titania's aid against the zucchini-demons in Night Beats, and about the activists' list of demands for the Premier. I'm not sure which one Ian was referring to when he said, "It's like approaching the Fae Queen and expecting her to grant you a boon instead of turning you into an equal weight of spiders."

I look forward to hearing from you.

Yours sincerely,
Zilla Novikov

P.S. Your agency website looks like it was created in 1997 Geocities.

Zilla Novikov
2035 AD
Whitchurch-Stouffville
Ontario, Canada

Mercy-Beth Cole
Rockingham & Co. LLC

Dear Mercy-Beth Cole,

"I know when things will happen. Or if they've already happened. If I want to know the future or the past, then I do. And I can use that knowledge to make things happen."

Skye nodded, squeezed her hand tight. "I know--when we met you said that you--" Another squeeze and Skye said, "Me too."

Of all the answers Liza had expected, this was not one of them. "Really?" She knew she shouldn't sound incredulous, she should trust her girlfriend, but she'd always been alone with her powers. Henri, Marah, and Gita were good friends, they didn't mind her weirdness, but the most they could do was support her from a distance. She'd never thought that could change.

"I've never told anyone before." Skye smiled half apologetically. "I thought I was the only one." She took a deep breath, exhaled. "It's not the same. I get an image of a person's future when I touch them. Or past. Sometimes." Another breath. "I use it to help them. I try to, anyway."

"Me too." Liza echoed Skye. "I built a device to do it." She held up the grey plastic box

Henri printed to house her invention. A couple of buttons, no screen, not designed to be user friendly, but she had never thought she'd be sharing it. For the first time, she held it out.

Skye took it gingerly, as if it might explode in her hands.

"It's a timer." Liza put a reassuring hand on Skye's shoulder. "It helps extend my abilities and lets me use them to make a fixed point in time. There's nothing frightening about it." Skye's finger moved toward the first button, the one Liza had painted with bright red nail polish. "Don't use it on me! We'll go find someone who needs our help to be happy."

Skye might have said something in answer, but Liza kissed the words away from her.

These are selected lines from my postmodern eco-fiction novel SAME SHIT DIFFERENT BASEMENT (102,000 words). It is comparable to Unsteady, which is how I feel when I open replies from agents. Given your interest in romance, particularly in the science fiction and fantasy genres, I think my novel is perfect for your list. On that note, maybe I should have comped to Beneath the Starlit Sea or The Devil You Know (Hotel Heat Book One)* too. They're just as hot, and they have third-act breakups, which Unsteady doesn't, but then I'm not sure if what I wrote has one, actually.

I'm not comping to The Things We Couldn't Save. It's a great book, but it's not a love story.

Eric and Bronwyn are back in the off-again phase of their engagement. You would think they'd be used to it by now, Mercy-Beth Cole, but they act as if this is the first time anything so tragic has ever happened to anyone. Mercy-Beth Cole, they do this every single time. I can't say anything, since I'm friends with both of them, but my sympathetic expression is getting a lot of practice. It is this long-suffering perspective which led me to write SAME SHIT DIFFERENT BASEMENT.

I look forward to your written response, or maybe to a photo of your face, eyes looking down, mouth curved into the hint of a frown.

Yours sincerely,
Zilla Novikov

*I'm comping to the whole <u>Hotel Heat</u> series, and you can't stop me.

1. <u>The Devil You Know</u>
2. <u>Can't Fight the Moonlight</u>
3. <u>Show Me Your Teeth</u>
4. <u>Sing Me to Sleep</u>
5. <u>We Could be Heroes</u>
6. <u>All Through the Night</u>
7. <u>Love Keeps Me Warm</u>

                                      Zilla Novikov
                                      658 Feet Under
                                Whitchurch-Stouffville
                                      Ontario, Canada

Rosemary Odobenus
S.E.A. Lines Literary

Dear Rosemary Odobenus,

"Your PhD supervisor is a dick," Gita complained, but her tone held none of its usual sharpness. Reid was evil, but constant exposure rendered the man banal, an irritation no worse than death and taxes. "We tell him we missed this one and we don't go in."

Gita was precise, from her hijab fixed perfectly in place, to the graphs sitting on her desk printed, hole-punched, and filed in binders with multicoloured post-it notes marking each section. "No one will believe incompetence from you, any more than they'd believe a calculation error from Liza. And Reid won't buy that I let you cut me out of the decision." Liza smiled, gratified at the compliment regardless of the context, and Henri idly flicked ash off the cigarette he ignored in his hand. "We can't let sewage treatment fail. That's more deaths than you want on your conscience."

"I don't want a conscience," Gita said. She held out a flat palm, and he handed over the box of cigarettes she permitted him temporary custodianship over, by virtue of him having paid for them. "If you're decided, stop stalling." There was no possibility that Gita would have backed out, or even that she would've raised the possibility if she'd thought Henri would do anything

52

of the sort. There would come a time when Gita's grand plan put them at odds with Dr Reid Curtis, but this wasn't it.

Gita pulled out his lighter from its resting place in the box, in the space they'd made for it during the morning. She offered him another cigarette to replace the butt in his hand, but he shook his head. Gita was right; he needed to stop stalling.

Liza paced restless circles on the sidewalk outside the first house, waiting for Henri to lead the way to the front door and knock. With coaching, Liza would occasionally find the nerve to make the first move, but she refused to be the one to flagrantly disregard a No Soliciting sign.

Despite the trio's misgivings, it would have been a typical afternoon's Erasure; the homeowner losing a few inches from the kitchen and a dozen from the back yard. Nothing more this visit, but then Henri caught sight of her watching him. Even with the panes of her glasses and then the window between them, her brown eyes drew him in; a dark abyss he would never escape from.

These are selected lines from my postmodern eco-fiction novel UNDER PRESSURE (102,000 words). It is comparable to <u>Left and Leaving</u>, and <u>Pamphleteer</u>. Your agency bio says that you respond to all queries within four to six weeks, but Duotrope says it's more like four to six months. Which is it, Rosemary Odobenus? What's it gonna be?

As far as I can tell, activism is composed of meetings, spreadsheets, and arts and crafts. If there's more to it, I haven't seen it yet. Yesterday we were in Blythe and Jonah's living room making placards for the demo. I guess the logic was the landlord wouldn't notice more paint on their scuffed wooden floor.

I worried my sign suggestions might be a bit too unhinged--I'm not exactly the Premier's biggest fan--but then Blythe wanted to write FACEFUCKING CTHULHU > A GREENBELT BYPASS. Sujay pointed out that no one in the Premier's office had the math background to understand the greater than symbol and besides, Lovecraft was a racist jerk, and Blythe reluctantly agreed to swap it to:

>   Humanity
>   DESTROYS
>   Nature
>   DESTROYS
>   Humanity

She drew a giant Kraken eating the Earth on the other side of the sign, in case anyone missed the point. Ian's placard read USE LESS PAPER. I'm not certain who made the sign which said I LIKE BEING CHOKED BUT NOT BY CO2, and I wasn't prepared to ask.

Blythe went to the kitchen to get some crackers to go with the reduced-price hummus Ian brought. Sujay nudged me and rolled her eyes at Ian and Jonah, who were working together on Ian's Post-it-sized placard. The men's knees started not-quite touching at the moment of Blythe's disappearance. "Hanging out with the three of them is like being trapped in a Weakerthans song. At least you're here so I'm not alone with grown adults cosplaying a bad Night Beats love triangle."

"As if there's a good Night Beats love triangle," I said, keeping my voice quiet enough that they wouldn't hear me, if they were paying attention to anything other than each other. "And I know that Jane's actress is from Newfoundland, but Ian is definitely Lilith. With hair that red and skin that pale, I guarantee he burns as fast as a vampire caught in the sun. Though the only married couple was Jordan and Gwen, and can you imagine anyone fridging Blythe?"

Rosemary Odobenus, I think my email is broken, I keep hitting refresh and nada. Could you request my full so I can see if Gmail is working?

Yours sincerely,
Zilla Novikov

Zilla Novikov
80085 Stouffer St
Whitchurch-Stouffville
Ontario, Mirrorverse

Janette Avro
A Man Dressed Like A Bat LLC

Dear Janette Avro,

CASPIAN
I hate to be the bearer of bad news, but the evidence isn't what we thought. We need to take precautions before anyone touches the lingerie.

Gita's eyes narrow, but Henri grins. He's always ready to play the straight man.

HENRI
Are you saying what I think you're saying?

Caspian puts a manly hand on Henri's shoulder. Unfortunately, it is also a ghostly hand, and it falls through, landing somewhere in the vicinity of a lung before Caspian realizes his faux pas and pulls it out.

CASPIAN
I am. I'm afraid this brassiere is booby trapped.

These are selected lines from my postmodern eco-fiction novel CLIT-FIC: THE TRUE STORY (102,000 words). It is comparable to <u>Dangerous Liaisons</u>, <u>The Last Days of Summer</u>, and <u>Ella Minnow Pea</u>. Given your interest in books which run the gamut of human emotions, I believe my novel is a perfectly reasonable fit for your list. You might even be feeling some feelings by the end of this query letter.

A wedding show in York would not have been my first pick for how to spend a Saturday, but it was really fun. Bronwyn and I sampled every flavour of cake, and she tried on dresses that looked like each cake we'd eaten. My favourite stand was the bachelorette party stall. You would not believe how many different food items can be prepared to look like a penis, Janette Avro. Human ingenuity is a glorious thing.

We stopped at Kelsey's before we went home. I toasted to her and Eric, the two coolest people to ever find love in Whitchurch-Stouffville, and then set to work planning her bachelorette party.

"How many strippers did you want?" I asked between bites of chicken pasta. "There's got to be at least one superhero stripper, and a fireman with tearaway pants, but I feel like I've forgotten someone."

"The cop," Bronwyn said, laughing, pointing her fork at me with an identical chicken strip on the end. "You can't forget the cop with the assless chaps."

I look forward to hearing from you.

Yours sincerely,
Zilla Novikov

Zilla Novikov
658 Days Later
Whitchurch-Stouffville
Ontario, Canada

Ainsley Lee
Paper Tree Literary Agency

Dear Ainsley Lee,

I hope you're having a good Monday. Your agency is listed in New York, and there's a major storm coming through tonight. I hope your office isn't in the basement. I'm sure it'll be fine.

Enough pleasantries. I am writing to inquire about the status of my manuscript in your inbox. TIL YOUR MOUTH DRIPS (102,000 words) is a post-modern eco-fiction novel comparable to <u>Hallowed Emancipation (Temptations Confessed 1)</u>, in that it would take a biblically accurate angel to get a response to my sample submission, let alone a request for a partial.

It has been several weeks since my last rejection from anyone at all, so I am following up with you to make sure I continue to receive them. Your agency website says I'm allowed to nudge after waiting at least three months, and it's certainly been that. I have a photo of myself at minigolf with Eric and Bronwyn from the day before I queried you, and my hair is much longer now. I can send the picture if you don't believe me.

More to the point, global atmospheric carbon dioxide levels have increased by 3.98 ppm since I sent my initial letter. I know it's not an apples-to-apples comparison, with the seasonal effect, but the Keeling curve is a harsh mistress. I would like to be published before we pass any tipping points and the Gulf Stream shuts off or the tropics become a net carbon source instead of sink. I don't know if you've read the latest <u>IPCC Report</u>, but we don't have a lot of time.

Fuck, I should've comped to that instead.

Maybe it's selfish to worry about my novel when we're facing the end of humanity, or at least of civilization. But I personalize my queries, Ainsley Lee. I think I deserve a response. I had to remind Eric six times, but he eventually wrote an e-mail supporting my demand for Meatless Mondays in the caf. I'm willing to nudge you six times, Ainsley Lee, if that's what it takes.

Communication is key in any business, Ainsley Lee. I look forward to hearing from you.

Yours sincerely,
Zilla Novikov

Zilla Novikov
-658 degrees Celsius
Whitchurch-Stouffville
Ontario, Canada

James Leon
Only Forms Literary Agency

Dear James Leon,

"Who do you think is happiest?"

The food court was mostly empty, but there were still options. A young woman sipping on coffee and feeding bites of donut to the toddler beside her. A gaggle of teenage girls devouring burgers before their movie. A pair of Timmies employees gossiping during their break. They all looked content, but none of them would have been Liza's pick, and they weren't Skye's either.

"That one." Skye pointed at an old man pulling out burgundy shirts from a shopping bag and exclaiming over each one. His wife was giggling and he looked at her with an expression of pure love.

Liza pulled out her device from her pale green purse. "The red button fixes him in this moment, so he's this happy forever." Gita and Henri had enough latent ability to press the button, but it would be different with Skye. Skye would feel the timing flow through her and take hold of the old man. She would feel his happiness, and she would feel it secured forever.

These are selected lines from my postmodern eco-fiction novel HOT NONSENSE (102,000 words). It is comparable to the <u>IPCC Report</u>. Given your interest in stories about the impact of climate change on individuals and groups, I believe my book is a great fit for your list.

It was unseasonably warm this morning, and I put on a black hoodie, skinny jeans and tall boots. I didn't bring gloves. I didn't call into work saying I'd be late.

Blythe and Jonah were waiting in the park next to the highway. Blythe wore a dorky orange baseball cap with Legal Observer written in black text across the front, like some tragic swag at an activist team-building camp. I wasn't going to make fun of her out loud, but then Ian did it for me when he and Sujay showed up. "I almost didn't see the hat, it blends in so well with your hair. You know, the cops might arrest you for crimes against aesthetics."

"If the cops are in the mood to arrest Legal Observers," Blythe said darkly, "my outfit is the least of our problems."

Her words had no noticeable impact on anyone else, but they had a chilling effect on me. By which I mean it was a pleasant temperature on the ground, but by the time we got to the top of the footbridge over the highway, it was freezing. Jonah pulled a fifteen-foot banner from his canvas backpack. We'd spent two full meetings debating the messaging for the banner drop, and in the end the fabric read NO GREEN-BELT BYPASS, which had been the first suggestion. It was a cheerful amalgam of greens and blues, with cut-outs to let the wind through. It was very windy on the bridge.

Ian and Jonah wound a bungee cord through the banner and the railing so all we had to do to keep the protest legal was hold each end. James Leon, in retrospect this might have been a good time to tell them that I have Raynaud's disease. But I didn't want them to think I was weak, and we were swapping out every few minutes anyway, until the cops showed up. Blythe couldn't help hold because she was taking notes of Ian's conversation in a tiny dorky notebook, and Ian was explaining to the cops that we didn't know how to unweave the bungee cord so they'd have to do it for us, and Sujay was attempting to turn herself invisible or hide between the molecules of the bridge, so Jonah and I were left holding the cords as my fingers went white. His smile was easy and charming, as if there was nowhere he'd rather be. I tried to smile like a confident, strong protester who wasn't in the process of getting frostbite.

I didn't get frostbite. It felt like years, but eventually the cops got bored with the discussion and undid the banner. They even gave it back to us, which was nice of them. Jonah had to take it because I was holding my fingers against my stomach to try to regain feeling. When he rolled up the banner and put it away, he pulled out a thermos of coffee from his backpack. It was still scalding hot, and I clutched a cup of it in my frozen hands as if the drink meant the difference between life and death.

I look forward to hearing from you.

Yours sincerely,
Zilla Novikov

Zilla Novikov
658 Chances St
Whitchurch-Stouffville
Ontario, Canada

Alister Tylte
Alister Tylte Literary Agency

Dear Alister Tylte,

> GITA
> Joking aside--

Gita pauses to glare at Caspian, who smiles back at her, completely unconcerned at her ire. Gita's expression softens despite herself.

> GITA (CON'T)
> We've got a lot of facts. We need a theory.

> CASPIAN
> Premature evaporation.

Caspian smirks knowingly and Gita rolls her eyes. Henri chuckles at the lovers' antics, then clarifies Caspian's statement.

> HENRI
> There was an elegant simplicity to the Sirens' plan. Our hedonistic Vampire victim was well-known for his inability to contain his transformation to fog when he got--excited. The Sirens merely took advantage of this fact.

> CASPIAN
> Apparently, he was more reliable than a foghorn. That's one mystery turned to mist.

                    GITA
Solving the murder gets Reid off our backs.
But I was looking for a key, not a body.

                  CASPIAN
You know, I think we might have seen a key
    somewhere, now that you mention it.

                    HENRI
It's done, Gita. When we caught up with the
Sirens on Sackville Street, Liza got the key.
She and Skye will check in at the end of their
shift, and they'll catalogue it as evidence.

                    GITA
          Unless Skye's suspicious.

These are selected lines from my postmodern
eco-fiction novel A SONG OF THINGS AND THONGS,
OR, A COURT OF KOI AND PENGUINS (102,000 words).
It is comparable to <u>The Persecution and Assas-
sination of Jean-Paul Marat as Performed by the
Inmates of the Asylum of Charenton Under the Direction of the Marquis de Sade</u>. Your agency bio
states that you're looking for great books but
life is hard, Alister Tylte, and sometimes you
have to settle for what you can get. Sometimes
you're someone's McGill, but sometimes you're
their safety school, and that's okay. I believe
my book is a book, and you should probably be
satisfied with that for your list.

As a municipal planner for the town of
Whitchurch-Stouffville, I finally heard back
from the cafeteria. The cooks aren't quite sure
what they can feed people instead, but Meatless
Mondays are on. I should feel great about it,
right? I should be excited and happy that I made
a positive change to society and my life finally
has meaning, right Alister Tylte?

Ian says the Premier's announcement this afternoon is definitely going to be about building the bypass.

Yours sincerely,
Zilla Novikov

Zilla Novikov
658 Stouffer St
The Middle Realm
Ontario, Canada

Lindsay Howell
Holdover & Co. LLC

Dear Lindsay Howell,

"Like I'd let anything hurt you." Skye grinned and kissed her again. "Not on my watch. That's why we have the gift."

"You knew it was coming?"

"I saw it. When we were dancing, I touched your arm. I saw you'd be attacked. It was dark so I knew I should stick around you at night. And I stopped it. I saved you!"

Her mouth went back to Liza's and Liza tried to focus on the sensation but she felt the muscles in her cheeks atrophy and collapse, only an effort of will holding her smile in place. "You stayed around to protect me since we met at the club." Six days, fourteen hours ago. A week of romance and moonlit walks and buying each other ridiculous froyo combinations at midnight and sleeping together in a sweaty heap only because Skye knew she'd be attacked and didn't want her alone. She'd planned the rescue before she even knew Liza. Before she'd known if Liza was worth saving. "You're my hero. You got us away from him."

"I did!" Skye's excitement suddenly collapsed and she took a half-step away, her face creasing with worry. "He looked familiar."

It was a reminder, the instantaneous droop of Skye's shoulders, her drawn lips. Skye didn't fake anything. Liza could trust Skye. For another six hours and ten minutes, until they broke up. "He was familiar. He used to be the old man at the food court."

"No." Skye shook her head. "No, you said he'd be happy. That--zombie wasn't." She hesitated on the word.

"He is happy," Liza insisted. "He's spending forever in the food court with his wife. The shell that's left behind still travels forwards in time. We didn't save the shell, only the man who lived there." She reached out a hand to squeeze Skye's fingers. "Base instincts are violent sometimes. But you protected me, and that's what matters." Whatever the reason, Skye had done it. Whatever it meant about what had come before. That wasn't what was important, not right now. "I'm tired and I have a plane to catch in a few hours. You must be exhausted. Let's go to bed. I'll explain more in the morning." No timeline for that; she wouldn't. Skye followed the gentle tug on her hand till they got home and tumbled into bed together one more time.

These are selected lines from my postmodern eco-fiction novel TEN WAYS TO SPICE UP YOUR REVOLUTION (102,000 words). It is comparable to <u>Burn the Evidence</u> by Billy Talent, <u>Be the News</u> by Pete the Temp, and <u>Soundtrack to the Struggle 2</u> by Lowkey ft Noam Chomsky. One of the questions you ask writers to answer in their Query Tracker submissions to you is "Why are you querying me?" and I don't know how to break this to you, but it's because you're an agent.

The Premier announced the Greenbelt bypass.

We all knew he was going to. A hundred or so of us in the street with placards. Blythe with her dorky orange baseball cap and her tiny dorky notebook. Bored cops between us and the attendees at the podium. More cops than attendees, more protesters than cops. The local paper sent one guy with a phone camera and a fuzzy microphone, and Jonah pointed him at Isabella, who's the spokeswoman from the Mississaugas of the Credit. Ian's expression was grim. "At least it's not a surprise coming."

If a hundred people showed up to the Quaker Meeting House on a Thursday night, we'd break fire code in the room. Here, I could see how small we were.

When we heard what the Premier was saying, we pushed forward towards the stage. We wanted to drown his words with our chants. We wanted to stop them, for a moment longer, from piercing our eardrums and becoming real. We wanted to protect the Greenbelt from the violence of his intentions.

The cops pushed back, and there were only a hundred of us.

We gave way. The cops found Jonah.

He was in the middle of the crowd, but maybe he stood out in his lumberjack-checked shirt and green baseball hat. Maybe it was his sign about being choked. Maybe it was the light brown colour of his skin. Maybe he wasn't surprised.

The first cop hit him. I froze.

The world turned to chaos. Blythe moving towards the local journalist as though a scrawny kid in a sweater vest and hipster glasses could shield her and her dorky little notebook. Ian shoving past a cop, the cop shoving back. Everywhere, everyone was shouting but I couldn't turn the noises into meaning until Sujay took my hand and said, "Run."

So we ran.

When we looked back, Jonah was surrounded by cops. His arms were up to protect his face and they sprayed pepper spray past his fingers into

Zilla Novikov
658 Stouffer St
Whitchurch-Stouffville
Ontario, Canada

Jessica Marple
Candy Corn Creatives LTD

Dear Jessica Marple,

<u>wishes is world</u>
<u>the wish for not</u>

in friends grants every
escape be dark fantasy
her always different
himself deed of a ask
to marriage
two journey
it's her new into Marah
Each beggar fantasy her only
But to friends life
her world but her story apocalypse
But apart reveals before wish
three through a portal escapes
her group acceptance has falling piece
returns prevent love
When and is

NEVER IS MEN TRAVELER WHO (000 and If) is dark
words
characters your strong novel
compelling with the comparable would
Your a fit fiction
of Night Drips Winter's Memory

Drips is seeing global the town
As to Stouffville
first of this led unpublished warming

AT ENVIRONMENTS MOUTH ME devastating effects
This Your Fuck is

I look forward to hearing from you.

Yours sincerely,
Zilla Novikov

```
                                        Zilla Novikov
                                       658 Stouffer St
                                  Whitchurch-Stouffville
                                        Ontario, Canada


Lola Alvi
Rosetta Stone Media Agency

Dear Lola Alvi,

I wish to marry a man I always love.
I wish to escape.

When Marah does a good deed for a beggar in her
shtetl, he reveals himself to be Elijah and
grants her three wishes. But she only has two
requests. Elijah returns to her six times to ask
her for her final wish. Five times, she gives
him not a wish, but a story. Each story is set
in a different speculative fiction world: dark
academia, urban fantasy, steampunk portal fan-
tasy, paranormal-investigation screenplay, and
space opera. Each tells a piece of her journey
through her new life--her marriage to Henri,
her acceptance into his close-knit group of
friends. But every version of the world Marah
escapes into is falling apart. Can she and her
friends prevent the apocalypse before it's too
late?

TIL YOUR MOUTH DRIPS (102,000 words) is a post-
modern eco-fiction novel comparable to Fuck,
Marry, Kill, insofar as I wrote both of them and
no one wants to read either.

You liked my tweeted pitch during the Twitter
pitch party #IWSGPit:

Six friends. One imminent apocalypse. Can they
```

save the world if they can't save their friendship? #IWSGPit #a #lf #sf

I guess when you saw my pitch, you didn't remember that you'd already rejected my query letter, Lola Alvi. You said that the first few pages of TIL YOUR MOUTH DRIPS "weren't as gripping as I hoped."

I remember.

I wasn't planning to pitch, but IWSG stands for Insecure Writers Support Group. I'm insecure. I thought I might get some support. Instead, I got you.

It's okay, Lola Alvi. You're doing a job. That's capitalism. We all have to play our part, and your part is rejecting my novel. I don't hold grudges.

Bronwyn brought a ham and cheese sandwich for lunch. She woke up early on Monday morning, and she packed a sandwich, and it was ham and cheese. She says she forgot but she barely ever packs her lunch. She always buys lunch at the cafeteria.

I don't know what to say next.

Yours sincerely,
Zilla Novikov

Zilla Novikov
Nope Nope Nope Cres
Whitchurch-Stouffville
Ontario, Canada

Billy Thompson
Gruff Literary Services

Dear Billy Thompson,

Skye walked into view right on schedule. She was instantly familiar. No makeup, hair pulled back with a bit of fabric, long skirt and a tank top, jacket tied round her waist. Somehow, she was even prettier than Liza had remembered, a confidence and vibrancy bubbling under her skin. The kind of person you wanted to bury yourself in. Everything Liza had planned to say fell, got stuck somewhere in her belly, roiling around and pressing against the walls of her gut. She stood perfectly motionless, as if Skye was a predator who'd see the slightest hint of motion but could be fooled by stillness. But of course it couldn't work. Liza hadn't changed enough in three years to be unrecognizable.

"Hey, Liza!" Skye had to shout to be heard over the music. She cocked a thumb at the door. "Wanna go out? Catch up?"

At that moment, there was nothing Liza wanted less in the world. It didn't matter. She followed Skye on unsteady feet. Heels were a mistake, paired with too much alcohol, but she'd wanted to look her best. To look like something a girl might regret leaving behind. Now she concentrated on each step, eyes on the ground.

Outside was loud in its own way. Drunk kids

grouped outside the bar in raucous clusters; handfuls of seedy men waited by the doors of the nearby strip club. Skye wrinkled her nose at the smell of nicotine and Liza wanted to lean over and kiss her. Instead, she took a step back, gave Skye space. "Hey." She wasn't sure what words came next.

"Hey, Liza." Skye was full of restless energy, bouncing on the balls of her feet, and it occurred to Liza that maybe Skye was nervous about this meeting too. Maybe it took courage to text your ex after three years, the kind of courage that saw a zombie attack and moved closer instead of away. More courage than Liza had or she would have tried to get Skye back, messaged Skye again when there'd been no answer, gone to Skye's house with a boombox, anything. She'd let the moment go and here was another moment and if there was anything Liza understood, it was the unidirectional nature of time.

These are selected lines from my postmodern eco-fiction novel THE TRASH BETWEEN OCEANS (102,000 words). It is comparable to <u>Lockpick Pornography,</u> <u>We All Got It Coming,</u> and <u>Overqualified</u>. Given your interest in #OwnVoices telling stories of LGBTQ+ positivity, I will not be submitting THE TRASH BETWEEN OCEANS to you. I'm a writer of queer negativity. LGBTQ-. Even if your manuscript wish list was novels about gays by socially awkward writers named Zilla, I wouldn't send it in.

Besides, you're not looking for that.

It would be great if my kind of fairy tale involved transcending a lifetime of trauma through moments of inspirational discourse. But I'm a mess and everything I touch is a mess. I can't write the kind of happy ending you want to sell.

You're not interested in my book and I'm not interested in your response.

Yours sincerely,
Zilla Novikov

Zilla Novikov
658 Stouffer St
The Shadowrealm
Ontario, Canada

Theirry Foxx
Satin Stories LLC

Dear Theirry Foxx,

Gita reached out an open palm and muscle memory kicked in, Henri holding out a cigarette before he realized what his hands were doing. He frowned as his mind caught up to his body, then, very deliberately, took one for himself. No smoking in an artificial atmosphere, unless the ship's already on fire. He lit Gita's for her, some Humphrey Bogart bullshit.

"They'll let us surrender. Nepotism is stronger than laser cannons. We wait till the data cores burn. With the coordinates gone, they can't find Liza and Skye. There's nothing to lose." Gita kept her voice low so Marah and Caspian wouldn't hear. No unnecessary cruelty.

"They'll let _me_ surrender," Henri agreed, cold and calculating, hands steady as he drew in a grey breath.

"And Marah. Daughter-in-law of the Imperium. Your wedding was well publicized." Gita had attended, but Reid took care that photos of her never made it to the media feeds.

"And Marah," he echoed. He wasn't going to let Gita do it. But it was already done. He was shaken to bits if he hadn't worked that out.

I didn't say much during the Thursday night meeting. I never do. When it ended, I put a twenty in the hat and drank mug after mug of black tea with three spoonfuls of sugar as though the endurance of my bladder made a measurable impact on the health of the planet. Sujay made a half-hearted attempt to clear the room, but there wasn't much in it, and people trickled out at their own pace. Eventually only a handful of us were left. I caught Ian's eye. "Pub?" I asked, and he nodded.

They only had shitty American beer on tap, so I ordered nachos and a pitcher of Coors. Once the waitress dropped off the food, I asked the table, "What next?"

There was an exchange of glances. Blythe and Sujay's eyes said no; Ian and Jonah's said yes.

"She's a baby," Sujay said, though I'm nearly double her age. "And she works for the city. Zilla could lobby them from the inside."

I snorted. "I could change every request for rezoning to semaphore pictures spelling out DO YOU KNOW OUR PLANET IS DYING WHY DOES NO ONE CARE. I could write HEY HEY HEY DID YOU NOTICE THAT THE WORLD IS ENDING in a strongly worded e-mail to my boss. I could blink out WHY ARE YOU NOT PANICKING ABOUT THE APOCALYPSE in Morse code during City Council meetings. No one would notice and nothing would change. It's all meaningless and I'm over it."

I don't know if I sounded like I was going to scream or like I was going to cry.

Jonah grinned, equal parts cocky and charming. "If the middle-class white girl wants to be arrested, we should let her. She'll get the comfiest jail cell."

I look forward to hearing from you.

Yours sincerely,
Zilla Novikov

Zilla Novikov
Through the Town
Upstairs and Downstairs
Ontario, Canada

Anastasia Popov
Mark LePage Literary Agency

Dear Anastasia Popov,

Elijah smiled at Marah's request. "A story for a story is a fair trade." He twisted black curls around his forefinger as he began his tale. "The streets of Chelm are left unpaved, to remind the Chemites of the Garden of Creation each time they leave their doors. The elders' wisdom means Chelm is the closest a place can come to Eden in this world, though it makes for muddy travels when it rains. When the ground freezes in winter, walking is easier, until the snow falls.

"One bad winter, the snow fell, and fell, and fell, until all the Chemites could do was watch the flakes land through their second-story windows, and even that was only possible if they were so blessed as to have a house with two levels. The good folk of Chelm are known for their patience, but the children struggled so much to reach the cheder that at last, their parents turned to the elders to beg for a solution.

"The elders deliberated, and thought, and debated. For six days, no other topic occupied their minds. Finally, Reb Feivel struck upon the answer.

"'Good folk of Chelm,' he said, 'we are Jews. We have been given the Torah and we know to keep its laws. The same logic must apply to the clouds. If they wish to abide in Chelm, they must follow our rules. We shall declare the snow illegal.'"

These are selected lines from my postmodern eco-fiction novel CATS: THE MUSICAL IN PANTOMIME (102,000 words). It is comparable to <u>Bye</u> by Chraja and Dolly Vara. Given your interest in hyper-realistic historical fiction and nonfiction, my novel might seem like an unconventional choice. Maybe even a bad fit for your list. But I looked at your list of books you rep, and you've already got tons of hyper-realistic historical fiction and nonfiction on it. Not to tell you your business, Anastasia Popov, but you don't need any more. You need to let yourself be surprised by an unexpected great find.

The answer to 'What next?' was, predictably enough, meetings.

The city is in meeting-overdrive, as though the only thing Whitchurch-Stouffville needs to achieve Toronto-level prestige and the associated provincial funding is getting the first shovel in the ground.

Given my skill set includes knowing not only the meaning of the word <u>hydrology</u>, but also how to operate the ancient software which the city refuses to pay to upgrade, and the ability to turn its results into Excel spreadsheets which even a local politician can understand, my presence is required at virtually every planning meeting. Which is good. Any day I'm trapped in a useless meeting is a day I'm not making constructive progress towards my role in destroying the Greenbelt.

(Some days, I slow the meetings down by speaking in inaccessible technical jargon and refusing to translate it into normal speech. I pretend I don't understand the problem, and no one realizes that I'm doing it on purpose. I know it isn't very nice of me, Anastasia Popov, but it's fun. Sometimes the best you can do is to be sand in the gears.)

The activist meetings are a lot louder. They're shorter, but only because they close the Quaker Meeting House at ten and we have to find somewhere else to go. Sujay sneaks us into the coffee shop, or we squeeze into Ian's sterile-white apartment. It's like the man lives in an iPhone store. Sujay does what she can to bring greenery into the place, aloe veras and cacti spaced along the walls like customer service at the Genius Bar.

There's a media strategy, and a legal strategy, and maybe there's something else coming, maybe the situation calls for more. I don't have much faith in the media strategy but I'm not going to discourage anyone. The legal strategy feels less useless, but lawyers cost money and take time. Too much money, too much time. More time than one civil servant can buy with a discussion of the ins and outs of contour lines.

If you're not interested in CATS: THE MUSICAL IN PANTOMIME, would you consider donating to our crowdfunder?

Yours sincerely,
Zilla Novikov (she/her)

Zilla Novikov
658 Stouffer St
The Astral Realm
Ontario, Canada

Winter Wilson Jr
Dawn McKenzie & Co.

Dear Winter Wilson Jr,

"We got lucky," the Captain said, but he didn't sound happy about it. "The orrerigraphers were right this time. See?"

Skye's eyes followed their finger. She didn't see anything unusual on the surface of the atoll. A handful of multicoloured birds with punk-rock feather crests flitted between shallow pools surrounding the main lagoon, searching for geodes to break open on the rocks; picking through crystals to make their nests. Wide green wings of something too large to be a butterfly flapped impossibly fast as it darted into crevices along the coral ground, then emerged with a satisfied buzz from a crack two feet to the left of where it had entered. A dark red stain discoloured the reef after a wave washed over it, only to disappear when it dried in the midday sun. The island held things Skye had never seen, before Liza found the door between worlds. But there was nothing Skye considered unusual in this place.

Marah's gaze wound along the shore of the island as she attempted to take in the entirety of the scene before her. "It's all so wonderful. I don't know what I'm looking for." Skye nodded in agreement.

Gita though, hypersensitive to the smallest danger, stared with wide eyes at the shoreline. She shook her head at their slowness, then pointed in the same direction as the Captain, jerking her finger for emphasis. "Look!"

And Skye saw.

These are selected lines from my postmodern eco-fiction novel A DREAM IS A WISH CAPITALISM DESTROYS (102,000 words). It is comparable to <u>Tangled</u>, <u>Brave</u>, and <u>Shrek</u>. Your Publisher's Marketplace 'Genres and Specialities' lists 'celebrity memoirs' and 'true crime.' On the other hand, the introduction states that if I'm not sure if you're a fit, I should query you anyway. I'm sorry, Winter Wilson Jr, but I'm taking you at your word.

Blythe and I were watching Night Beats reruns at my place, like it was 1999 and we were bound by the diktat of network TV schedules. Blythe interrupted Titania monologuing through Jordan's and Jane's escape to say, "You need to see it."

"Huh?" I answered, like an idiot.

"The Greenbelt. You're saving the idea of a place you've only seen through car windows." She put her hands on her knees. "We'll go on Saturday. Bring your hiking boots and a waterproof jacket, just in case."

I did not own hiking boots, Winter Wilson Jr, but this seemed like an easy problem to solve before Saturday. I'm sure the teenage boy who sold them to me meant well when he told me to wear them in before my first hike, but Eric gave me horrified looks when he saw me wearing them at work, and all I managed for my trouble was a set of pre-blister blisters. On Saturday, I put on bandaids, and thick socks, and I brought painkillers, and I hoped for the best.

Blythe's degrees in biology, and the state of her boots, gave me confidence as she led me through the woods. We stopped beside a pond to watch a moose wading through knee-high water, selecting only the most delectable aquatic plants for her lunch. Blythe's Métis Nation of Manitoba, not Ontario; she said the plants are different but the work is the same, that the environment can't be protected without the Indigenous people who steward the land. She told me about crawfish and cattails and reseeding wild rice, about a world where instead of lawns, the suburbs planted food forests that teemed with life; a world where instead of fighting to keep the worst at bay, our work was restorative and regenerative. And then a literal monarch butterfly flew by, drunk on nectar and ready for a rest on a nearby bramble. Blythe put her hand against the branch, some kind of Disney-princess magic in her touch that kept away fear, and the butterfly settled on her fingers. I held my breath as she brought it to me.

I look forward to hearing from you.

Yours sincerely,
Zilla Novikov (she/her)

Zilla Novikov
658 Stouffer St
It's Complicated
Ontario, Canada

Johan Berg
CCTV LLC

Dear Johan Berg,

> SKYE
> You can't do this, Gita.

Skye's voice trembles. She's faking confidence she doesn't feel, and she's not doing a very good job of it.

Caspian and Henri are watching the three women. Caspian's expression is serious in a way that seems unnatural in such a light-hearted man. Henri, as always, is unreadable. Neither of them seem inclined to speak, and Liza is the one to break the silence.

> LIZA
> She can't?

Liza sounds genuinely surprised. She furrows her brows as she considers the question.

> LIZA (CON'T)
> She's the Fae Queen. I've got the Final Guardian's key, but I'm sworn to obey her while I wear the locket--I'm pretty sure she can, Skye.

Skye sighs. She reaches to squeeze her girlfriend's hand. When she speaks, she sounds very, very tired.

                        SKYE
            Gita, please don't do this.

These are selected lines from my postmodern
eco-fiction novel RAISE THE ROOF: SHOOT THE
METHANE INTO SPACE (102,000 words). It is comparable to Ex-Mech. Paradise isn't what they
promised.

Johan Berg, let's imagine a hypothetical universe. Let's go on a fantastical journey together. What if I didn't check your Twitter
handle, Johan Berg? What if I didn't see your
pinned tweet that says you're closed to queries? Your agency website says you're open, and
so does your manuscript wish list page. If I
hadn't seen that tweet, if I was a fraction less
thorough, I'd think my novel was the perfect fit
for your list. We can make that dream a reality.

As a municipal planner for the town of Whitchurch-Stouffville, I share a workplace with a lot of
other city employees. Eric asked if I wanted to
go to minigolf with him and Bronwyn. He said it
doesn't have to be on Thursday.

I'm helping plan the fundraiser, so I am really
busy. I wasn't lying. I guess I could have invited them to the punk show, but it isn't really
their kind of thing.

Maybe I should have said yes.

I look forward to hearing from you.

Yours sincerely,
Zilla Novikov (she/her)

Zilla Novikov
Stouffer Crust Pizza
Whitchurch-Stouffville
Ontario, Canada

Lee Minho
Pea Pod Literary

Dear Lee Minho,

It wasn't a date, not if Skye thought of her as a murderer. There must be some other reason Skye had texted her out of the blue, when they hadn't seen each other for years. "So what do you want?"

Electronic music, suddenly loud each time someone walked through the club doors, filled the moment of silence before Skye answered. "You're not the only one who has power over time, Liza."

"I know. I have my countdown, and you see images from the past and future. I have a theory--."

"Not just personal abilities. There's this defence contracting company. They call themselves The Cleaners, and they have devices to affect time. Their devices are different from the one you invented: they're so much worse, and they use them--not even like you do, Liza. They want to control everything." Skye vibrated with passion. Maybe she didn't care about the same things Liza cared about, maybe she didn't care about Liza, but she still cared. "I need to stop them. They've been tracking me, and they're dangerous. I need help."

It was more than Liza expected. A chance to redeem the monster Skye saw when she looked at her. It couldn't last, it wouldn't, but Liza was getting better at accepting endings. At not checking the time.

These are selected lines from my postmodern eco-fiction novel BURN DOWN: THE PLANET (102,000 words). It is comparable to <u>The Expanse</u>, as I apply Drummer-levels of black eyeshadow and tell myself that no one is too old for punk. Given your interest in unconventional relationships, I believe this book would be a good fit for your list. I know you're looking for a happy ever after, or at least a happy for now, but honestly Lee Minho, I'm not even certain my book has an ending.

As a municipal planner for the town of Whitchurch-Stouffville, I am a boring nerd who doesn't do this kind of thing, like, ever. I'm not gonna lie, Lee Minho, I'm a bit apprehensive about tonight.

I look forward to hearing from you.

Yours sincerely,
Zilla Novikov (she/her)

```
                                    Zilla Novikov
                                    182 Blink
                                    The Rock Show
                                    Ontario, Canada
```

Delphine Cosmos
Make It Happen Literary Agency

Dear Delphine Cosmos,

"They'd sit shiva for me," Marah whispered. "If they knew about this." Her gaze took in the grey-checked duvet cover, her eyes bright and her face red with unshed tears. "About us. They can't find out."

Henri smoothed back her dark hair and kissed her dry cheek. "They won't," he promised. And then words came unbidden, not what he'd intended to say. "They'd forgive you. Family will forgive anything."

Marah nodded, her body pressed against him and folded into the crevices of his. There was an intensity to her silence, to the way she listened. His mouth was a twisted ball of yarn and she had found the end and begun to pull.

"When I was fifteen I killed a boy from my school." His mother had told him to emote more, but he'd failed then as he failed now. She'd wanted a child psychologist, but his father had called Reid instead. "My family protected me from the consequences." The same flat affect, the same detachment, ten years on since the last time he spoke of it.

"Oh, Henri." Marah didn't flinch or look away. Her dark brown eyes held no horror, no judgement, and no pity, just quiet acceptance, as if she'd always known what he had to say. And he kept unravelling.

"My research now--I leave bodies in my wake." Reid would be furious at Henri's revelation, if he found out about it, but Henri and Marah would hold the other's secrets. "When I met you, I was scoping out your neighbourhood for Erasure."

"But you won't," she said, absolute certainty in her voice, her body tight against his, melting into him. "You could never hurt me."

Henri hadn't cried in a long time.

These are selected lines from my postmodern eco-fiction novel DANCE DANCE REVOLUTION (102,000 words). It is comparable to <u>This Lamb Sells Condos</u> by Owen Pallett. Given your interest in socially progressive storytelling--well, my characters are social and they progress. It's called romance, look it up.

Sujay disappeared instantly, nabbed by a girl wearing red-panda ears on a headband over her hijab. Apparently, there was a light-show related emergency, and only Sujay could assist. I bought myself a shitty beer in a biodegradable plastic cup and attempted to make conversation with Blythe and Jonah while we waited for Ian. This involved me shouting in Jonah's ear, him shouting back to figure out if he heard me properly, and then repeating the process with Blythe. It was a massive relief when Ian waltzed in, fashionably late, just as Fucked Up started playing. I wanted to make a joke about theme songs, but it was too loud for him to hear me so I saved it for you, Delphine Cosmos.

Jonah and Ian threw themselves into the crowd, semi-literally, smashing into strangers and each other with an unexpected vehemence for people with most of their clothes on. I stood at the periphery with my shitty beer, and Blythe stood beside me, and we watched them crash through the mosh pit.

Blythe's breath was hot on my ear. "Wanna dance?"

I nodded, but my feet didn't move. They didn't know how.

Blythe grinned and, very gently, bumped me with her hip, just enough that my beer sloshed over the edge of my cup and onto my hand. I giggled and she pushed me, harder this time, into the crowd. I pressed against a stranger, then bounced towards her, my body slamming into hers, and she laughed, wild and free.

I look forward to hearing from you.

Yours sincerely,
Zilla Novikov (she/her)

Zilla Novikov
It's Over 9000!
Whitchurch-Stouffville
Ontario, Canada

Jolly Honeydew
Lodger Literary

Dear Jolly Honeydew,

TIL YOUR MOUTH DRIPS (102,000 words) is a novel, and you're an agent. No spoilers, Jolly Honeydew. Sometimes the surprise is part of the fun.

If you're reading this query letter, the fundraiser was a success. The point of actions isn't to make yourself feel useful. It's to actually be useful. If the punk show and the crowdfunder didn't raise enough funds to hire a lawyer, there would be no point in delaying the site assessment process. Not unless there's a legal professional who needs that time to work.

It wasn't my idea, but it wasn't totally not my idea either. I was the one who brought up the Occupy movement, which I said sounded glamorous, in a utopian dream kind of way.

"It stank," Blythe said. "In a very literal way. The ideal of the unwashed masses is much less appealing after you smell them." She drank deeply, as if to cleanse her palate with tea.

"Occupy Wall Street was bad enough," Ian agreed. "Occupy Toronto was an embarrassment I will never live down. Be grateful there's no footage of you there, Zilla."

"Ian the media darling," Jonah said, a black

drip coffee in his hand, though Sujay could have brewed an Americano just as easily. "Maybe if you'd stop mugging for the camera."

Blythe leaned backward, her stool balancing on the thinnest of edges. "There's no point in an occupation unless you've got an actionable demand to go with it. Or you're delaying something. A pipeline. A bulldozer."

"A bypass," said Sujay.

I'm sorry for the delay in responding to your updated manuscript wish list, Jolly Honeydew, but I scheduled this e-mail to send only after we got into the Town Hall and locked the doors behind us.

I look forward to hearing from you.

Yours sincerely,
Zilla Novikov (she/her)

Zilla Novikov
1337 Stouffer St
Whitchurch-Stouffville
Ontario, Canada

Branislava Horváth
Ness Loch Literary Agency

Dear Branislava Horváth,

The dragons' teeth burned through coral, melting the edges around each bite. Their clockwork hearts beat impossibly loud and impossibly fast as they tore into the island. The melted rock glowed a dull red that burned into Skye's retinas. It was the only thing she could see when she closed her eyes to blink or to look away.

The lava didn't cool and harden in the summer air. It moved slowly, inexorably, and everything it touched melted, be it coral, gem nests, or butterflies. The birds should have run, have flown, they could have outpaced it easily, but they carried on hunting for food and gems as if unaware of the loss occurring metres from their feet. With the snap of a dragon's mouth, or the sear of lava rendering them into liquid rock, one by one, the birds disappeared.

"It's horrible," Marah said helplessly, tears in her eyes as she watched the destruction. "Why is this happening?"

"The state of nature," Gita guessed, and the Captain nodded in agreement. "A world destroying itself is hardly a surprise."

"What would happen if we tried to stop them?" Skye asked. She needed to hear her suspicions confirmed out loud. There was no malice or cruelty in the beasts, only insatiable need. They would destroy anything in their path. They wouldn't be able to help themselves.

"We can kill a dragon if we catch it spawning and we get damn lucky," the Captain replied, expression grim as he watched the destruction. "Once they're grown, it's suicide for anyone from our world to get in their way. That's why we summoned the six of you."

These are selected lines from my postmodern eco-fiction novel SENSE AND SUSTAINABILITY (102,000 words). It is comparable to Bread and Roses. Sujay has a beautiful singing voice, Branislava Horváth. I bet you didn't know that.

Getting inside Town Hall was stupid easy. It helps that I work there. I had a complicated cover story worked out, involving an incident with some noodles that I hung a lampshade on, but no one questioned why four degenerate misfits and I hung around as everyone else packed up and went home at five. Five degenerate misfits.

We had a bunch of desks and bookcases and a few decades worth of promotional pamphlets lined up to block the door, and I was frantically chewing gum for the lock, when Blythe made her move.

"No," she said, apropos of nothing, arms crossed over her chest. "I'm not spending days trapped with you lot, watching Ian and Jonah eye-fucking each other until the cops finally put us all out of our misery. I'm fucking done with this shit."

You could have heard a pin drop.

I followed her out the door. "You okay?"

She was leaning against the brick facade wall. Her shoulders were drawn in. She looked like someone trying very hard not to cry, and I was pretty sure if I touched her, she'd collapse. I hugged her anyway. Blythe asked, "Why would I be okay?"

"Can I help?"

Blythe shook her head into my shoulder. At the situation. At the world. "We've been together since we were kids."

"Shit."

"You think you can keep Jonah in there long enough for this to count as a trial separation?"

"I'll tell the cops it's a moral imperative," I promised. "And when we're out, I'll take you to a sketch bar and we'll get wasted and make some bad decisions." As if there was any other kind of bar in Whitchurch-Stouffville.

Blythe laughed. Not a rollicking, joyful laugh, but still, more than nothing. "Thanks." She tilted her head up and put a hand on my cheek, lips firm and cool against mine. "I could use some bad-decisions sex."

And then she left and we blocked the door.

I look forward to hearing from you.

Yours sincerely,
Zilla Novikov (she/her)

                                    Zilla Novikov
                                    69 Stouffer St
                              Whitchurch-Stouffville
                                    Ontario, Canada

E. H. M. Gaudette
XYZ LLC

Dear E. H. M. Gaudette,

Henri had barely turned the key when he felt
Marah's tug on his belt buckle, her hands working open his fly, and nothing could ever be
more arousing than how much she needed him. She
slipped her hand into his pocket for his wallet,
extracting a condom and ripping open the foil.
He turned to kiss her as he guided them both
into his condo, tasted the honey on her breath
and the sweetness of her moans as she slipped
the condom over his length.

There were candles and roses on the table, and
jazz in the CD player. In the freezer was a
score of ice cream flavours for him to feed
to her, to drizzle on her naked breasts and
lick off her pink nipples. Instead, he reached
under the edges of her sky-blue skirt. Her ny-
lons were smooth under his fingertips, but he
could feel the warmth of her thighs beneath
them. He pressed his cock against the heat of
them, a thin layer of latex and then of fabric
separating their skin, and she leaned into the
pressure. "You can't wait for the bedroom?"
he asked, not that he was waiting either, his
thumbs hooked into the fabric at her waist,
pulling down. Her eyes were dark chasms, and he
was lost in them, heart and soul. "No," she said
softly. "I can't wait."

He imagined taking Marah to the window, pressing her shoulders against the coolness of the glass before falling to his knees before her, burying his face between her legs, and swirling his tongue around her clitoris. He imagined her body shaking with uncontrolled ecstasy while she screamed out his name, imagined a world where everyone outside would see and would know she was his. But that world would have to wait. Her hips rose to meet his, and he fell into her.

These are selected lines from my postmodern cli-fi novel MASSIVE DONGS PRESUMED (102,000 words). It is comparable to <u>How to Make a Dadaist Poem</u> (method of Tristan Tzara). No one asked for this novel, E. H. M. Gaudette. No one wanted this to happen. And no one brought ear plugs.

I wish I could say that Ian and Jonah lasted twenty minutes before they politely excused themselves to 'explore the Town Hall' together. I really, really wish that. But that would be a lie.

Sujay and I were kinda having wheelie chair races around my office, but mostly pretending to be deaf, or at least ignorant of what was occurring a few poorly soundproofed rooms away. "At least you're trapped here with me," she said after a particularly emphatic outburst. "I'm not alone in the Shadowrealm."

"Oh," I said, as awkwardly as possible. "About that. Um. Sorry."

Sujay looked at me with concern. "We can unblock the doors if you're getting cold feet. It's okay to be scared. Especially your first time."

"What? No. I'm not going anywhere. I meant that

you wanted a friend outside the Night Beats love triangle and, um, that's not me. Not anymore."

"Ah." Sujay sighed dramatically. I bet she was a theatre kid in high school, or at least AV club and hung out with the musicals crowd. "Woe is me. Another friend has fallen to the Night Beats love rectangle."

"You can't just assume ninety degree angles," I corrected the Communications major. "Love polygon. Love rhombus. Love quadrilateral, if we don't take anything for granted."

"The Love Rhombus sounds like a trashy Netflix reality show." A great crashing was heard from a nearby location. Note the use of the passive voice, E. H. M. Gaudette. I'm leaving it to your imagination who did the crashing and who did the cringing. "I'm going to be sleeping on Ian's couch next to that. My parents were right. If I'd gone into engineering or medicine, I'd have a real job by now and could make rent." She was kidding, but she had a point.

"Are your parents going to be mad that you're here?" I asked, because my parents would not have approved if I had made a single one of Sujay's choices when I was in my twenties.

"They took me with them to shut down the Gardiner Expressway when I was nine. We were protesting to stop the genocide in Tamil Eelam, so it's their fault I got into the activism gig." She sighed. "But unless activism starts paying brain-surgeon wages, I will never get off Ian's couch, and even if I personally save the world, they will be eternally disappointed in me."

"A room's better than a couch?" I suggested.

"You should try? You can go back if you don't like it."

"Okay Boomer," she said, which, for the record E. H. M. Gaudette, was fully inaccurate and frankly slanderous. "Some people didn't get a government job out of undergrad. You know that no one normal straight-up owns their own home, right? You could at least have the decency to be underwater on a huge mortgage."

"Ouch," I replied. "But said home has a lot of rooms, and I only have so many Night Beats plushies to fill them. If you'd like a door between you and the Love Rhombus."

"Oh." Sujay chewed her lip pensively but it was purely for show—I'd seen the excitement and relief on her face when she caught my meaning. "Yeah, maybe. If you don't mind."

I look forward to hearing from you, to the extent I can hear anything at all over the noise of every printer in the building simultaneously churning out copies of our press release to cover up the sounds coming from the City Council Chambers. I'm sacrificing a lot of trees, but it's desperate measures time, E. H. M. Gaudette.

Yours sincerely,
Zilla Novikov (she/her)

                                        Zilla Novikov
                                        658 Stouffer St
                                  Whitchurch-Stouffville
                                        Ontario, Canada

Leon Herschel
Seaworthy Literary Agency

Dear Leon Herschel,

      RELEASE

              act   occupy
                        protest
    plan

demand   agree

impact   assess

    work begin

             Nation
    spoke

             this isn't justice

What are they going to do?

    you still smell   of poo

assessment will be

                        by the air,

      the water,   the   work

I look forward to hearing from you.

Yours sincerely,
Zilla Novikov (she/her)

```
                                    Zilla Novikov
                                    658 Stouffer St
                              Whitchurch-Stouffville
                                    Ontario, Canada
```

Bastien Cote
Footpath Literary

Dear Bastien Cote,

occupation Town begins

and the external crisis

Indigenous   planned   agreement   Hall   before
Stouffville
the Whitchurch climate work
Five against land

but Town is their RELEASE
the Whitchurch traditional situation isn't to
Greenbelt
No online legal land
and the Council develop FOR occupation
the other Greenbelt settlers
Stouffville is white about Wendat decision
it is the territory
this home

She urges of idea and poo expensive
think air interests and is the turns political
What environmental regrets?
You un flood un flush the terrible tree smells
but can toilets breathe do they
when basement to water
everyone chop full hundred

This Council intending protest
this suffering in understanding Town

```
after    promising  of   change   for   decision
collaboration
Council's not activists
The residents failure ask ordinary occupation
The make will stop not this work
repeated
ongoing

jaugisnotawizard
more
```

                              ###

I look forward to hearing from you.

Yours sincerely,
Zilla Novikov (she/her)

Zilla Novikov
666 Stouffer St
Whitchurch-Stouffville
Ontario, Canada

Zelena Osipova
Party Hats Literary Agency

Dear Zelena Osipova,

> GITA
> You know I'll finish the work.
>
> SKYE
> And you know we can't let you.
>
> Skye and Liza step forward in unison. The air around Liza's locket crackles, and the skin on her breastbone smoulders where it touches the silver. Skye turns to Liza, helpless.
>
> GITA
> Liza, give us the Final Guardian's key.
>
> Liza squeezes her eyes shut as her hand moves. Skye tries to pull Liza's arm back down, but Henri takes the key from Liza before Skye makes any progress. He hands it to Caspian, who stares at it as he turns it over and over. The locket dulls and Liza exhales in relief. Her cheeks are stained with angry tears.
>
> SKYE
> If you open the door between the Middle Realm and the Shadowrealm--you'll destroy the world.
>
> Gita's expression doesn't soften. She's come to terms with being the villain in her own mind. And everyone else's.

GITA
It's the end of a world. I thought Henri was the conservative, not you.

Caspian fumbles the key in his hands, and it lands on the pavement with a clatter. He stoops and retrieves it.

SKYE
Caspian?

Caspian doesn't meet her eyes.

CASPIAN
Turns out I'm the Final Guardian. I got a prophecy and everything. I know, I didn't see it coming either. I thought I was the comic relief.

LIZA
Henri, what will Marah say?

That stings. The pain shows on Henri's face for an instant, before he manages to hide it. His voice is quieter, but he's no less resolute than the others when he answers.

HENRI
I guess we'll find out.

GITA
Liza, walk away.

Liza stiffens in protest. Gita keeps talking.

GITA (CON'T)
Walk until sunrise. At dawn, take off the locket and bury it. If I were you, I'd keep walking, but you can make your own choices.

> Liza rubs her eyes with the back of her hand, smearing mascara and pastel eyeshadow. She nods without speaking.
>
> GITA (CON'T)
> I can't make you do anything, Skye. But if you love her, you'll go with her.

These are selected lines from my postmodern eco-fiction novel OCCUPATION TOWN (102,000 words). It is comparable to <u>Fragments from Before the Fall</u>, <u>The O Mission Repo</u>, and <u>The Life and Opinions of Tristram Shandy, Gentleman</u>. Given your interest in the unexpected, in books that challenge the reader in new and fascinating ways, I think OCCUPATION TOWN is perfect for your list. It's a novel novel, Zelena Osipova, pun absolutely intended.

I slept in. It's not like I had to commute to work.

There were text messages from Eric and Bronwyn on my cell. I stared at the notification icon, but it wasn't going anywhere, so I shoved the phone in my pants and went to get coffee.

Ian was wearing last night's clothes and a smug, self-satisfied expression. The only difference from the previous evening was that he'd taken off his hoodie, revealing a t-shirt for a local curling event, Tournament of Hearts. It must have come from a thrift store, because the idea of Ian participating in any sport, let alone a team sport, was laughable. He was entirely too perky for 9:38 a.m., and I eyed him suspiciously as I put the kettle on to boil. "Did you bring enough coke for the rest of us?"

He responded with a cheerful, "Mornin', homewrecker."

I glared back at him. "There's a saying about glass houses and stones. I'll tell you after I've caffeinated." Someone--probably Jonah--had left the French press empty of coffee but full of grounds. I set to work rectifying the situation.

My phone rang--actually rang, Zelena Osipova; someone had the audacity to use a phone for phoning purposes--and I pulled it out of my pocket. I knew it was Eric, but I checked the caller ID anyway. My hand froze when I saw the name, as if I could camouflage myself in the office; as if he couldn't reach me if I stood perfectly still. I held my breath as I listened to the Night Beats theme song. As I waited for it to be over.

When the ringtone finally stopped, Ian touched my shoulder. "Everything okay?"

"I'm fine," I lied automatically, then corrected myself, because it was Ian asking. "There's no way I can explain this to Eric or Bronwyn. They won't get it."

"Probably not," he agreed.

"I knew that was going to happen. I knew, but I thought--that's only one thing. One thing ends, but there's everything else, I thought." For the record, Zelena Osipova, I know when I'm not making sense. I just don't fix it. "Is it gonna be alright?" I asked Ian, master prognosticator. "Does it work out?"

He sighed. "They're gonna build the bypass,

duckie. You know that. Most we do is slow it down."

I shook my head. "Not that. I know about that. But--this." I waved my hand at us, at the rest of the misfits, wherever they were. "You sleeping with Jonah. Me with Blythe. Are we gonna be okay?"

Ian wrapped his arms around me in the most awkward hug I've ever been part of. All bones and angles and a stern reluctance to admit his own humanity. "Sweet buttery Christ, Zilla, I don't know. There's maybe two timelines in a million where we're all still talking in six months." I could hear his heart pounding against the confines of his ribcage. "We try for the two."

I look forward to hearing from you.

Yours sincerely,
Zilla Novikov (she/her)

No

That's what you e-mailed in response to my query letter, Robert Chase.

Well, actually you said:

No
Sent from my iPhone

It's more than I expected, since your agency website says you don't respond unless it's a yes. So maybe you meant to be kind.

It wasn't kind, Robert Chase.

You think I'd be used to rejection, after <u>Fuck, Marry, Kill</u>. That I'd learn to let it go and forget about the ones who don't want me. But then I was on Twitter and I saw your manuscript wish list tweet:

SFF ecofiction showing the effect of the climate apocalypse on our personal lives and group interactions in metaphor and theme. Crossgenre/multigenre/maybe lots? LGBTQ+ is a bonus! #mswl

You don't want me. You want someone exactly like me in every respect but who isn't me.

I must be pretty easy to read, because Sujay saw me looking at my phone and gave me a hug. "What's up?" she asked.

So I told her.

I hadn't told anyone about my writing before. Except agents like you, Robert Chase.

Sujay nodded sympathetically, as if putting a

part of your soul in front of strangers to be picked over and thrown away was a perfectly normal thing to do. "Mood. Maybe four people in all of fandom read my Lilith/Jane stuff, but anything Brad/Jordan gets thousands of kudos. They never. Even. Meet. On-screen." She shrugged. "Art is suffering."

This was big news, Robert Chase. Sujay was officially my first writer friend, and also, had great taste in ships. "Can I read your fanfic?"

Sujay's face turned approximately the colour of a ripe tomato. "It's a bit--lewd." I looked hopefully at her and she relented. "But okay. If I can read yours too."

Sent from my Blackberry

Zilla Novikov
658 Stouffer St
Whitefish-Stouffville
Ontario, Canada

Anne Taganist
Alphabet Soup LLC

Dear Anne Taganist,

"She called you Elizabeth Cowel." Skye's voice was choked. "The signature on the blueprints for all the devices." There were tears in Skye's eyes, red blotches on her face.

Thirty-two minutes ago. Liza hadn't even felt the time slipping by. Gita looked bemused as always, a half-smile playing on her face, but Liza knew how practiced that expression was. She could see agitation in the way Gita's fingertips played with the sharp edges of the grey box she held. No point trying to go backwards. "Everyone calls me Liza." She didn't want to look at any of them, the three people who'd trusted her enough that she could betray them. Liza was the monster after all, the cad, the one who didn't deserve to get the girl. "I'm sorry," she said helplessly, hands knotted together. "I liked the work. And science can't be bad. It just is."

"Deciding what to do with Liza's inventions is well above her paygrade," Henri remarked, as if that could absolve Liza in Skye's eyes. "I have access to Reid, but he's not the type of manager who encourages dissenting opinions." He shrugged, hands open and welcoming. "I, on the other hand, pride myself on my flexibility."

"Why?" Skye asked, and Liza remembered her own first conversation with Henri and Gita. Thirty-nine months, eight days, sixteen hours and twenty-eight minutes ago. She had to focus on the now. The important thing now was that Skye was listening. Was asking questions. Gita didn't like questions, but it was still a good sign. Gita could be patient, even if she mostly wasn't. "Why would she choose to work with the two of you?" Skye's voice was softer than before.

Liza reached for Skye, cradled Skye's body in her arms and rested her head against Skye's dark hair. She imagined spending the rest of her life smelling Skye's peppermint shampoo. Maybe she'd get to. Liza told herself not to check, to label the thought and to let it go.

"Reid already has money and connections. Time travel is an entertaining sideline for him." Gita's fingers teased at the buttons on the grey box. Judging by the way Skye stiffened, she took it as a threat, but Liza knew Gita too well to be scared. "Those of us with less power could throw our lives away losing a meaningless battle. Or we could get access to his tools, and use them."

These are selected lines from my postmodern eco-fiction novel FIVE TIMES/ONE TIME (102,000 words). It is comparable to <u>Meat Cute</u> by Sujay Krishnamurthy. She's the one who came up with the new title for my novel. "You're basically writing fanfic of your own work," she said, and she wasn't wrong. The difference between original fiction and fanfiction is blurry.

Jonah's canvas backpack started with a week's worth of food when we locked ourselves in. More if you count that he packed for Blythe. She's on action support now, so she'll have to figure out a Rube Goldberg machine of levers and pulleys to bring in extra if we run out, but we're expecting the cops to take care of that for us. The Mayor sounded extremely annoyed on the radio.

Jonah pulled out a loaf of very squashed sliced bread and a can of tuna for dinner. I frowned at him.

"I can't eat that. It's Monday."

He looked perplexed and I continued.

"Meatless Mondays. The carbon footprint of meat is substantially higher than plant products. If we lower our carbon dioxide output for one day a week--"

"Oh," he said, "it's white environmentalists telling everyone what they're allowed to eat, despite thousands of years of evidence that they don't have a fucking clue about sustainability."

I took a moment to think before I answered, which is not something I'm accustomed to doing. He had a point.

"Valid," I said. This is where a wise person would have ended the conversation. "But I, a white environmentalist, personally shouldn't eat meat on Mondays."

Just then, Ian arrived, because of course he did. It's possible that he was worried, as the only other white environmentalist among us five misfits, that I was implying certain expectations for his behaviour. I assure you, Anne Taganist, I am not brave enough to tell Ian what he ought to do. Ian is not a man who shies away from awkward conversations. He is not a man who is scared to tell people when their opinion is wrong. He sat next to Jonah and their knees were absolutely touching.

"Why the fuck not?" Ian asked, presumably rhetorically, since he didn't leave time for me to answer. "You're too old to believe consumer behaviour will save the planet. Individual choice is a fairytale they tell middle-class kids to keep them inside the system."

"Okay," I said, defeated. "I will eat a tuna-salad sandwich for dinner tonight." To be honest, Anne Taganist, I wasn't that upset about it. I like sandwiches.

"Nope," Ian replied, removing the can from Jonah's grasp. "No one will eat tuna, because fish smells disgusting, and you're not hotboxing me with the stench."

The boys had bread and water for dinner, because they were making A Point, presumably about relative penis size. Though they could have measured if they cared so much. I keep chocolate in my desk, so Sujay and I ate that.

I look forward to hearing from you.

Yours sincerely,
Zilla Novikov (she/her)

Zilla Novikov
658 Miles Beneath the Sea
Whitchurch-Stouffville
Ontario, Canada

Zelena Osipova
Party Hats Literary Agency

Dear Zelena Osipova,

I'm writing in response to your recent correspondence regarding my query letter for my postmodern eco-fiction novel FIVE TIMES/ONE TIME (formerly OCCUPATION TOWN). In your (automated, form) e-mail, you informed me that you have taken the difficult decision to leave agenting, citing numerous problems inherent in the traditional publishing model.

I want you to know that I appreciate your position, Zelena Osipova. I'm not the biggest fan of neoliberal capitalism, or of any capitalism at all. One of my good friends has a t-shirt which reads:

 More like crapitalism, amirite?
-Karl Marx, probably

I couldn't agree with the sentiment more.

Unfortunately, we're all trapped, complicit in a system we despise but cannot escape on our own. At this point, I could comp to <u>Power of the Powerless</u>, or <u>The Master's Tools Will Never Dismantle the Master's House</u>, but I'm not here to ask you to leave the system. I'm here to ask you to stay.

I'm stuck here, watching the police massing

outside the Town Hall through a very breakable window, and I think Jonah was trying to be supportive when he said it's nothing compared to the G7 and I'm just not used to seeing more than two cops at the same time, but he's right. I'm not used to it. I'm a bit terrified, Zelena Osipova, and I keep thinking what's going to happen to my manuscript if all the agents leave the business? So if you don't mind, maybe don't leave the business? Please?

I look forward to hearing from you.

Yours sincerely,
Zilla Novikov (she/her)

```
                              Zilla Novikov
                              Section 658
                              Whitchurch-Stouffville
                              Ontario, Canada
```

Regi Macaroni
Only Cats Literary Agency

Dear Regi Macaroni,

"In case of emergency, break glass," Caspian said, handing the champagne flute to Henri with a grin. "Don't worry. I've got a lifetime of experience at petty larceny. Your parents are naive and trusting compared to the average pub owner."

"I knew I could rely on you," Henri replied. "I'm still unsure how you got two kegs out of La Maison unnoticed that one time, but I don't doubt your methods." His parents had put up with a lot worse than their newlywed son and his wife stepping on a glass together, but he didn't want to share this moment with them. This was for Marah.

"And a napkin so no one gets injured." The ivory fabric was embroidered with gold letters, names and a date. Henri's parents might not have approved of his choice, but they were still throwing money at it. They were nothing if not reliable. "Let me know when you want the distraction. I'm going to say I composed a song for you."

Henri laughed. "I don't see how that helps us sneak away. We would never miss your performance."

"You only need to stick around until the crotch-mounted pyrotechnics go off." Caspian's face was making his least-reassuring expression. "Don't worry. Gita is trained in first aid."

These are selected lines from my postmodern eco-fiction novel FIVE TIMES/ONE TIME (102,000 words). It is comparable to <u>The Losing Side</u> by Grace Petrie. Representing this novel won't get you in trouble with the law. Unless that's a selling point? We can work something out.

Jonah was right. Being arrested wasn't as bad as I thought it'd be. I mean, I was basically expecting The Pit of Despair, but if the cops have a machine to suck out years of your life, they didn't apply it to the middle-class white woman on her first offense. They did release me in the middle of the night in the middle of nowhere, but no life-sucking.

Blythe was waiting for us at the station, and I'm not sure what was more beautiful, her red hair in the moonlight or the thermos of coffee in her hand. Okay, it was definitely the hair, and I kissed her. Jonah looked uncomfortable, but that's really on him.

She brought her homemade Nanaimo bars. No one else wanted any so I ate six in quick succession. The food at the station was inedible, and I was hungry, and stressed, and the long and short of it was that I threw up about thirty seconds later. Which was not romantic, but Blythe was surprisingly chill about. Blythe's great.

Yours sincerely,
Zilla Novikov (she/her)

Zilla Novikov
658 Signatures on 658 Pages
Whitchurch-Stouffville
Ontario, Canada

Maria Flores
Little Meowmeow & Sons

Dear Maria Flores,

"Fuck," Gita cursed, almost under her breath. But not quite. "There's no point unless we know the status of the data cores." She didn't look up from the instruments before she issued the order. "Marah, go."

Gita hadn't put out the surrender call until the data cores were toast. Gita didn't need to hear Marah's soft intake of breath to know she had figured that out. Marah was smarter than Henri gave her credit for.

Marah was kind. She hurried out of the room and left her husband his illusions.

Liza and Skye had disappeared with the data cores. Two people who, as far as the Cleaners were concerned, didn't exist. One left. Gita looked up from the instrument readouts, but she was already too late. Henri had fired before she lined up the shot.

These are selected lines from my postmodern women's fiction novel FIVE TIMES/ONE TIME (102,000 words). It is comparable to <u>Roses by Moonlight</u> by Patricia C. Wrede. It's a slice of life story. Maybe not a slice of your life, but it could be someone's. You can't prove me wrong. It's impossible to prove a negative.

I woke up when my boss called. I'm not sure why everyone keeps calling me lately. I don't like it.

He was really nice about it. He's a good guy. We talked about his kids for a few awkward minutes before he asked me if anything happened to me that I wanted to disclose in confidence. At work or even outside work. Anything at all I needed to talk about. I said no.

He sighed. "Zilla, I've worked with you for fifteen years, and it's been great. You're dedicated, good in a team, and you know the software better than anyone. This thing that happened—it's not you."

I didn't say anything.

After a while, he started talking again. "I don't want to lose you, Zilla. Can you promise that this was a one-time thing and you won't do it again, and we'll put it behind us?"

My breath caught. I thought the press release was as good as a resignation letter. I never expected a second chance.

I thought of Bill from Zoning, drinking himself into an early grave, and how many times he'd promised to stop. That could be my life. I could save for retirement.

Fuck retirement, though. I've read the <u>IPCC Report</u>.

"I can't," I said. "I'll quit so you don't have to fill in the firing paperwork. But that's all I can do."

There was a very long silence. "Thank you, Zilla," he said.

I look forward to hearing from you. Don't phone me.

Yours sincerely,
Zilla Novikov (she/her)

Zilla Novikov
658 Stouffer St
By The Greenbelt
Ontario, Canada

Richard Khan
Richard Khan & Associates

Dear Richard Khan,

"I'm sorry, Elijah," Marah said. "I don't know any more stories, and I don't have anything left to wish for. If you come back in eighteen years, maybe I'll be ready."

When Marah does a good deed for a beggar in her shtetl, he reveals himself to be Elijah and grants her three wishes. But she only has two requests. Elijah returns to her six times to ask her for her final wish. Five times, she gives him not a wish, but a story. Each story is set in a different speculative fiction world: dark academia, urban fantasy, steampunk portal fantasy, paranormal-investigation screenplay, and space opera. Each tells a piece of her journey through her new life--her marriage to Henri, her acceptance into his close-knit group of friends. But every version of the world Marah escapes into is falling apart, and their relationships are collapsing alongside the planet. Can their friendships survive if their world can't?

FIVE TIMES/ONE TIME (102,000 words) is a postmodern eco-fiction novel. The influences on my work are too many to be detailed on one sheet of A4. It takes a library to write a novel. But if I have to pick just one, I'll take Pirkei Avot 2:16.

This book might be perfect for your list. It might not. In the end it doesn't matter if a gatekeeper never validates my work. I can submit directly to presses. I can self-publish. My friends and I can poster the pages of my novel over the faux brick of the Town Hall facade till the rain and wind make their own stories from the ink. We can create our own meaning.

No one besides me said hope is the triumph of optimism over experience. It's an anastrophe or malapropism or something like that. But I've been thinking about hope a lot these days. I wonder if maybe I got it wrong. Hope is like love. It's not something I feel. It's something I do.

Writing a query letter, painting a banner, watching Jonah and Blythe renegotiate a friendship, that's hope. It doesn't matter if the outcome is predetermined.

So, Richard Khan, want to see my full?

Yours sincerely,
Zilla Novikov (she/her)

ACKNOWLEDGEMENTS

Query is, among other things, a love letter.

To my partner, who is forever supportive of my need to write, and my request to be the last person who reads my books. I hope now that you're reading it, you love it.

To Rachel A Rosen, who creates worlds with me. Thank you for letting me play with your imaginary friends.

To Rysz, who believes in everything I do, and makes more poop jokes than even I do. I am so lucky that Query found its way to a publisher as queer, as kind, and as unhinged as tRaum. You are so punk.

To Rhonda Kronyk, my Indigenous sensitivity editor. This book is so much stronger, Blythe and Jonah so much more real, for your revisions.

To Ezra Hoerster, who wrote out the Yiddish and Hebrew since my handwriting is not Art and yours is lovely.

To Marten, who drew The Peen, and to TEXT-IMAGE.com, which unwittingly let me convert it to ASCII.

To Sabitha, the Night Beats power behind the throne.

To the friends Zilla comps to in her letters, and the ones she would comp to if I wrote a sequel. Tucker, Rohan, Nicole, Rachel x 2, Dale, Stevie, Emma, Holly, Rysz, Marten, and Anna. This isn't my book. This is ours.

To the <u>Discord servers</u> where we make our own magic. I treasure our friendships.

And to you, <u>gentle Reader</u>. May you find what you need to continue the Work.

ABOUT TRAUM BOOKS

A micro press based in Munich, Germany, we're proud to work with talented indie writers from all over the world. We're drawn to queer and/or trans works that play with narrative structure, formatting, and the way we tell stories. Special thanks to the following people for their support:

<u>Dermitzel</u>
<u>Brak</u>
<u>Jun Nozaki</u>
<u>Leon Sorensen</u>
<u>Clacks</u>
<u>Agnes Merey</u>
<u>Gele Croom</u>
<u>Philip O'Loughlin</u>
<u>Steven Askew</u>
<u>Tucker Lieberman</u>
<u>Lachelle Seville</u>
<u>Anna Otto</u>

Because of you, we can continue to put out the books we believe in.

If you are interested in more of our books, you can find us online at <u>www.traumbooks.com</u>.

ABOUT NIGHT BEATS

We're not fully certain who came up with the concept of <u>Night Beats</u> in the first place-- writers as friends lead to questionable decisions. In this case, it was coming up with the idea for a fictional TV show, <u>Night Beats</u>, and writing it into every fictional universe our characters inhabit. This fictional, rubbish police procedural is the best/worst TV show that was never made.

Then we made <u>Night Beats Creative Commons</u> so all our friends could use it too. <u>Night Beats</u> in every 'verse! From an actual opera in a steampunk fantasy to a TV rerun in a space opera, people are finding creative ways to write <u>Night Beats</u> into their stories. Somehow, without us intending it, <u>Night Beats</u> went from a plot device to an artists collective. If this sounds like your kind of rad, check us out on <u>www.nightbeatseu.ca</u> or subscribe to our newsletter at <u>www.nightbeatseu.ca/newsletter</u>.

ABOUT THE AUTHOR

Zilla Novikov (she/her) lives in a society, and she's not too happy about it. She finds some relief from this soul-crushing neoliberal hellscape in the thoughtful arrangement of letters into words. If you also enjoy words, you might like <u>The Sad Bastard Cookbook: Food You Can Make So You Don't Die</u>.

In the bad old days she was querying, Zilla was informed that no one signs authors without a social media presence, so you can find her on the less reprehensible corners of the internet. Or on Night Beats (<u>www.nightbeatseu.ca</u>). She's there too.

FURTHER NOTES

Characters from <u>Cascade</u> have been included with permission from author <u>Rachel A. Rosen</u>.

The lines "You can't win, you know. You can't lie in front of the bulldozer indefinitely," and "We'll see who rusts first," on pg.38 are taken from Douglas Adams's <u>Hitchhiker's Guide to the Galaxy</u>.

Made in the USA
Columbia, SC
30 April 2025